Samuel French Acting Edition

The Canter

by Tim Kelly

SAMUELFRENCH.COM   SAMUELFRENCH.CO.UK

FOR PRODUCTION ENQUIRIES

UNITED STATES AND CANADA
Info@SamuelFrench.com
1-866-598-8449

UNITED KINGDOM AND EUROPE
Plays@SamuelFrench.co.uk
020-7255-4302

Each title is subject to availability from Samuel French, depending upon country of performance. Please be aware that *THE CANTERVILLE GHOST* may not be licensed by Samuel French in your territory. Professional and amateur producers should contact the nearest Samuel French office or licensing partner to verify availability.

THE CANTERVILLE GHOST

A Two-Act Play

For Fourteen Women and Six Men

CHARACTERS

JENNIE . . . . a maid at Canterville Chase
MRS. UMNEY .the housekeeper
LADY CANTERVILLE . . . . the former owner
WEEDS . . . . the gardener
PAM . . . . ,. . . . American teenager
WENDY . . . . .her sister
MRS. OTIS [LUCY] . . . . . .new owner of Canterville Chase
MR. OTIS [HORACE] . . . . .her husband
VIRGINIA . . . . Lucy's younger sister
SIR SIMON . . . . 'The Canterville Ghost'
VICAR . . . . village clergyman
LORD CECIL . . . . Lady Canterville's nephew
MRS. DAMPIER . . . . .vicar's wife
MADAM BALAKLAVA . . . . a 'psychic researcher'
MARTIN THE MANIAC . . . . a ghost
HESTER THE HORRID . . . . another ghost
LADY JOAN THE GRAVELESS . . . . .a ghost, too
VAMPIRE DUCHESS . . . . still another ghost
MRS. MIDWINTER . . . . a villager
MRS. MUSGRAVE . . . . another villager

TIME: The present.
PLACE: An old English manor house.

PRODUCTION NOTES

The set may simply be drapes or have a few representational flats. However, if space is limited, the DR room entrance can be placed off-stage; the same with the French doors. They can be suggested by having the characters look off-L whenever the garden is mentioned. The UC entrance will be UR, and the drapes which mask the 'walled room' will be off-RC. If there is no place to hang the portrait of Sir Simon, merely put a small frame on the table to suggest a 'miniature.' Ideally, however, a more effective setting can be created by utilizing the floor plan shown in the back.

Lightning is merely the stage lights flicked several times quite quickly. A good thunder effect can be achieved by hitting a sheet of metal with a hammer. There are also sound effects records for this.

The 'meringue pie' Madam Balaklava receives in the face is easily approximated by filling a paper plate with meringue. If Madam Balaklava can wear glasses the humor can be heightened by having her wipe them off separately and dramatically as she exits.

THE CANTERVILLE GHOST

ACT I

Scene 1

SCENE: A sitting room in Canterville Chase, an English estate.

AT RISE OF CURTAIN: JENNIE, a young maid, is standing at the open French doors looking into the garden. MRS UMNEY, a proper sort of housekeeper, enters DR carrying a vase of flowers.

MRS UMNEY. Any sign of them?

JENNIE. Not yet, Mrs. Umney. *[Turns]* If I was them Americans I wouldn't come here. I'd get on the first plane and fly straight home. *[MRS UMNEY moves to the table and puts down the vase]*

MRS UMNEY. You're a silly girl, Jennie. I don't know what you mean.

JENNIE. You know what I'm talking about. *[Fearful]* **Him.**

MRS UMNEY. You can't mean our gardener, Weeds?

JENNIE. *[Annoyed]* No, Mrs. Umney. I'm not talking about Mr. Weeds. I'm talking about Sir Simon. *[Hushed tone]* The ghost.

MRS UMNEY. *[Looking at the portrait]* The less said about him, my girl, the better.

JENNIE. You think Her Ladyship has told the new buyers about Sir Simon?

MRS UMNEY. It's not our place to speculate. *[Studies the portrait]* I do hope he'll behave.

JENNIE. Scared me half to death one night, he did.

MRS UMNEY. I thought you never saw him.

JENNIE. Never have. But I heard him coming up the stairs in his suit of armor, rattling his chains.

5

MRS UMNEY. *[Stares at rug]* I hope they won't notice the stain on the rug.

JENNIE. They're bound to see it. And ask about it.

MRS UMNEY. If we say nothing, they may suspect nothing.

[LADY CANTERVILLE enters in time to overhear this last remark]

LADY CANTERVILLE. That would be dishonest, Mrs. Umney.

MRS UMNEY. Good morning, M'lady.

JENNIE. We was discussing the ghost. *[LADY CANTERVILLE moves DS and studies the spot on the rug]*

LADY CANTERVILLE. Blood red. Nothing will wash it out.

MRS UMNEY. Canterville Chase won't seem the same in the hands of strangers, M'lady.

LADY CANTERVILLE. With taxes and all, I can't afford to keep it up. Mr. and Mrs. Otis are giving me a marvelous price.

JENNIE. And I may be giving notice.

LADY CANTERVILLE. That isn't sporting of you, Jennie. It wouldn't be cricket to leave the Americans without some staff. At least in the beginning.

MRS UMNEY. Besides, every member of your family has been in service here.

LADY CANTERVILLE. Go along, Jennie. See that there are fresh towels on the washstands.

JENNIE. Yes, ma'am.

[JENNIE exits]

MRS UMNEY. *[Turning to LADY CANTERVILLE]* How large a family, ma'am?

LADY CANTERVILLE. Two girls, teenagers. One is a year older than the other. Mrs. Otis' sister will also be in residence. I appreciate your staying on, Mrs. Umney. It'll make things easier for the Americans.

MRS UMNEY. I think of Canterville Chase as my home, Ma'am.

LADY CANTERVILLE. *[Looks to portrait]* Happily, you
and Sir Simon seem to get on.
MRS UMNEY. I always speak respectfully of him. Perhaps
he appreciates that.

*[WEEDS enters from French doors, wipes off his
cap]*

WEEDS. They're comin' up the path now, M'lady.
LADY CANTERVILLE. How very punctual.
WEEDS. I don't think Sir Simon is going to like strangers about
this place.
LADY CANTERVILLE. That's enough, Weeds. Go help with
the luggage. *[Voices from garden. All react, look L.
WEEDS steps R]*
PAM. Hurry up, Wendy. You're always lagging behind.
WENDY. I'm hurrying as fast as I can.
MRS OTIS. Slow down, girls.

*[PAM, a teenager wearing jeans, bounces through the French
doors. She and her sister, WENDY, are lively and extro–
verted]*

PAM. Oh, sorry. I didn't mean to burst in on anyone.
LADY CANTERVILLE. Quite all right, my dear. You're Wendy,
I imagine.
PAM. No, I'm Pam.

[WENDY enters via French doors, also wearing jeans]

WENDY. And I'm out of breath.
LADY CANTERVILLE. Then sit and rest.
WENDY. I'm not that tired! *[Impressed]* Are you Lady Canter-
ville?
LADY CANTERVILLE. I have that honor.
PAM. You're the first lady we've ever met.

WENDY. She means lady, you know — with a **title**.
LADY CANTERVILLE. I quite understand. *[To WEEDS]*
The luggage.
WEEDS. Yes, Madam.

[WEEDS exits]

LADY CANTERVILLE. I hope you girls will enjoy living
here.
PAM. It's terrific. *[WENDY moves UC taking in the room]*
WENDY. I'm going to love it here.
LADY CANTERVILLE. I hope so.
WENDY. Going to be great fun exploring.
MRS. UMNEY. Exploring, Miss? *[WENDY crosses to drapes]*
PAM. She's got this crazy idea she wants to be an archae-
ologist.
MRS. UMNEY. What on earth for?
PAM. Like digging in the earth, in old ruins, covering herself
with dust. Stupid if you ask me.
WENDY. No one's asking you. I'm going to investigate
every room in this place.
MRS. UMNEY. Not **every** room.
WENDY. What's behind the drapes?
LADY CANTERVILLE. It's a walled-up chamber.
PAM. That's exciting!
WENDY. Who walled it up?

[MRS. LUCY OTIS enters via the garden]

LUCY. I asked you girls not to charge ahead. What will Lady
Canterville think?
LADY CANTERVILLE. *[Stands]* I think they're charming.
*[LUCY moves to LADY CANTERVILLE. MRS.UMNEY
moves behind the sofa]*
LUCY. You're a diplomat, Lady Canterville. It takes one where
my daughters are concerned. I'm hoping a good English

Boarding school will calm them down.
PAM. We don't want to go to boarding school.
LUCY. That's one reason why you're going.
WENDY. Boarding school. Yeech!

[LUCY's sister, VIRGINIA, enters from the garden.
She's an intelligent young woman, pretty and alert.
She's followed by MR. HORACE OTIS]

HORACE. Lady Canterville. How nice to see you again. Didn't
keep you waiting, I trust.
LADY CANTERVILLE. Right on time. *[Nods to MRS. UMNEY]*
This is Mrs. Umney, the houskeeper I spoke of. *[HORACE,*
VIRGINIA and LUCY nod]
MRS. UMNEY. I bid you welcome to Canterville Chase.
PAM. Chase? Who's Canterville and who's he chasing? He'd do
that as a gallop, anyway!
MRS. UMNEY. Canterville Chase is the name of this place.
Chase is an old English word that means manor or lodge.
PAM. *[Embarrassed]* Oh.
LADY CANTERVILLE. *[To MRS. UMNEY]* I think we'll
have tea now.
MRS.UMNEY. Yes, M'lady.

[MRS. UMNEY exits DR]

LADY CANTERVILLE. *[To VIRGINIA]* You're Mrs. Otis'
sister.
VIRGINIA. A pleasure to be here, Lady Canterville.
LUCY. Forgive me. I forgot you two hadn't met.
LADY CANTERVILLE. Please sit down. I wanted to speak
to you one last time before we signed the final papers.
HORACE. No problem, I trust.
LADY CANTERVILLE. That would depend entirely on what one
means by a 'problem'.
LUCY. I don't follow.

LADY CANTERVILLE. I have not cared to live in Canterville Chase myself since my grand-aunt, the Dowager Duchess of Bolton, was . . . 'frightened' . . . into a fit.

VIRGINIA. Frightened?

HORACE. A fit?

LADY CANTERVILLE. A fit from which she never fully recovered.

LUCY. What frightened her?

LADY CANTERVILLE. Two skeleton hands were placed on her shoulders as she was dressing for dinner.

PAM. *[Delighted]* Wow!

WENDY. Skeleton hands! Way out!

LADY CANTERVILLE. I feel bound to tell you, Mr. and Mrs. Otis, that the ghost has been seen by several living members · of my family. *[The announcement has no adverse effect on the Americans, which rather baffles LADY CANTERVILLE]*

HORACE. Sounds marvelous to me. Local color, eh?

LUCY. Better than we hoped for.

VIRGINIA. Who is the ghost?

LADY CANTERVILLE. *[Points to portrait]* Sir Simon de Canterville.

PAM. Was he wicked?

LADY CANTERVILLE. Infamous. A villain and a scoundrel.

WENDY. Great!

LADY CANTERVILLE. None of you, I fear, realize the gravity of the situation. Sir Simon is not to be taken lightly.

HORACE. Ghosts don't mean the same thing to Americans as they do to the English. What we ought to do is catch Sir Simon, cage him, and sell him to a circus. People would pay to see a caged ghost. *[Americans laugh. Sound of thunder]*

VIRGINIA. That's odd. Thunder on such a lovely day.

LADY CANTERVILLE. Sir Simon has a habit of darkening rooms and causing thunder when he's displeased. I think

he took exception to your remark about putting him in a
cage. *[They try hard not to laugh again. All this 'ghost
talk is a bit much]*

HORACE. I'm sure we'll come to terms with Sir Simon.

LADY CANTERVILLE. After the unfortunate accident with
my aunt, most of the servants left. Except for Mrs. Umney,
of course. She has a certain feeling for the spirit world.

LUCY. There's a maid, too, isn't there?

LADY CANTERVILLE. Jennie. However, I have doubts
about her staying.

HORACE. Put your fears to rest, Lady Canterville. This
house is exactly what we're looking for.

LUCY. Exactly.

HORACE. We'll take it, spook and all.

LADY CANTERVILLE. *[Alarmed]* You mustn't refer
to Sir Simon as a .spook.

HORACE. If he shows up we'll confront him with good ole
American know-how. He'll soon learn to keep his place.

LADY CANTERVILLE. If you don't mind a ghost in the
house, it's all right with me. Only, you must remember —
I warned you.

HORACE. We'll take our chances.

LADY CANTERVILLE. Splendid. If you'll excuse me, I'll
get the final papers.

HORACE. *[Stands]* Of course.

[LADY CANTERVILLE exits USC]

PAM. That's the best news I've ever heard!

WENDY. Our own private ghost!

VIRGINIA. What a strange story.

LUCY. Lady Canterville's not the sort of woman who would
lie.

HORACE. Oh, she believes in what she says. Up to a point.
I bet there isn't a manor house or a castle or *[Pause,
grinning at PAM]* a chase, in England without a resident

ghost floating about. Helps sell property.

VIRGINIA. Then you don't believe her story?

HORACE. Because we're Americans, Lady Canterville probably
thinks a ghost will cinch the deal. She's awfully anxious
to unload the place.

WENDY. Reverse psychology.

HORACE. Precisely.

PAM. I was hoping it was for real.

HORACE. Take my word for it. If there's a ghost here, it
will turn out to be a whistle of wind in the bell tower.

[WEEDS appears at French doors]

WEEDS. Beg pardon, governor. I'll need the keys to the car
trunk.

HORACE. *[Pulls out his car keys]* I forgot I locked it.
You're Weeds.

WEEDS. That's right, governor. George Weeds. Finest
gardener and yardman hereabouts.

VIRGINIA. Weeds? What a wonderful name for a gardener.

WEEDS. It was my father's name, too.

[MRS. UMNEY enters DR]

MRS. UMNEY. China or Ceylon?

LUCY. *[Pauses]* How's that?

MRS. UMNEY. The tea.

LUCY. The China, I think.

MRS. UMNEY. Very good, Madam. *[She turns to exit]*

VIRGINIA. *[Sees the blood stain]* What on earth is that?

LUCY. I'm afraid something has been spilt.

MRS. UMNEY. *[Turns back]* Yes, Madam. Blood has spilt
on that spot.

AMERICANS. Blood?

VIRGINIA. How horrible.

HORACE. *[Steps C]* I must say you're putting on a good show,
Mrs. Umney.

MRS UMNEY. I speak the truth, sir.

LUCY. I don't care for blood stains in a sitting room. It must be removed at once.

WEEDS. Won't do no good, Mrs. Otis.

VIRGINIA. Why not?

WEEDS. *[Scared]* It's the blood of Lady Eleanor.

WENDY. Who's Lady Eleanor?

WEEDS. Sir Simon's wife.

MRS UMNEY. Died of a broken heart. Sir Simon's wickedness drove her to an early grave.

WEEDS. Nothin' will take out that spot.

LUCY. Nonsense. A drop of lighter fluid will take care of it. *[Stands]* Horace, hand me your lighter. *[He gives lighter to LUCY]* And your handkerchief. I'll only use a corner. *[He hands her a handkerchief, She wets a corner, kneels down and begins to rub at the stain. Dialog continues through this business]*

MRS UMNEY. That blood stain has been admired by tourists.

WEEDS. It's somethin' of a local attraction.

MRS. UMNEY. *[Positive]* **Nothing** will take it out.

LUCY. Rubbish. *[MRS. UMNEY steps closer. All watch as LUCY rubs away]*

VIRGINIA. I've never seen a red that vivid.

WEEDS. That blood stain don't talk, but I've heard things in this house that would make anyone's hair stand on end.

HORACE. We all like a bit of fantasy, Weeds. But there's no need to overdo it.

MRS UMNEY. It's no joke, Mr. Otis. The ghost is real.

WEEDS. Don't do to mock Sir Simon. He's got a nasty temper.

PAM. *[Points]* Look! The spot's disappearing.

WENDY. Almost gone.

LUCY. It is gone. *[Stands]* A little cleaning fluid and some elbow grease will fix a troublesome stain every time. *[Pleased with her work]* You may serve tea when ready, Mrs. Umney. *[MRS. UMNEY is amazed about the spot.*

LUCY gives lighter and handkerchief to HORACE]
MRS.UMNEY. In all the years I've been here, no one has been
    able to wipe away that stain.
LUCY. *[An order]* Tea, Mrs. Umney.
MRS. UMNEY. Yes, Madam.

   [MRS. UMNEY exits DR]

HORACE. And you can get the luggage, Weeds.
WEEDS. I don't believe me eyes. The stain's gone.
HORACE. But the luggage is still in the car trunk.

   [WEEDS exits into garden, scratching his head]

VIRGINIA. I feel guilty not appreciating all the trouble
    they've gone to.
LUCY. *[Laughs]* Blood stains on the carpet.
PAM. *[Laughs]* Two skeleton hands!
WENDY. *[Laughs]* Instead of a guest in the house, we have
    a ghost. *[All are laughing when, suddenly, the stage
    darkens and we hear a peal of deafening thunder]*
VIRGINIA. What's happening?
LUCY. *[Points]* The garden's all in shadows.
HORACE. Never saw a storm come up like that. *[All look
    into the garden]*

   *[SIR SIMON enters fast through the drapes in an
   absolute fury]*

SIR SIMON. Vulgar Americans! *[Horrified, terrified, all turn
    to see the ghost]*
PAM. The ghost!
WENDY. It's Sir Simon!
SIR SIMON. You have dared mock the spirit of Simon de Canter-
    ville! You will pay for your insults! Auuuuuuuuuuugh!
    [On his cry he charges after PAM and WENDY, who run

*screaming into the garden. VIRGINIA, in shock, flees
screaming. More thunder as SIR SIMON runs in pur-
suit of the girls, who are yelling, 'Help!' 'Help!' off-
stage. LUCY spins about and does a comic swoon
into her husband's arms]*

HORACE. *[To no one in particular]* Send for the U.S.
Marines! *[Very fast curtain]*

Scene 2

SCENE: The same. One week later, in the afternoon.

AT RISE OF CURTAIN: JENNIE is dusting at the sideboard. The vicar, REV. DAMPIER, enters from the garden.

VICAR. Morning, Jennie

JENNIE. Oh! *[Turns]* Oh, it's you, Vicar. Gave me quite a
start. Been away on a holiday, haven't you?

VICAR. *[Steps in]* My wife and I spent a week in London.

JENNIE. Enjoy yourselves?

VICAR. I'm afraid I'm much too fond of our village. All I
could think of was getting back here. Big city life is so
exhausting.

JENNIE. *[Moves C]* Sit yourself down, Vicar. I expect you'll be
wanting to see Mrs. Otis.

VICAR. *[Sits]* Mr. Otis, too – if he's about. I do feel guilty
not being here to greet them on their arrival. What
sort of people are they?

JENNIE. Awfully American. Would you have tea, Vicar?

VICAR. Very kind of you, Jennie. But, no.

JENNIE. I'll tell them you're here. I won't be long.

[JENNIE exits]

VICAR. Take your time. *[He looks at the portrait of SIR SIMON]* I do hope you're not causing any mischief, Sir Simon. Americans coming here could be a blessing for the village.

[VIRGINIA enters]

VIRGINIA. Jennie, oh . . . . *[She breaks off, seeing the visitor]* I'm Virginia Washington.   Mrs. Otis' sister.
VICAR. *[Standing]* And I am the Reverend Augustus Dampier. Vicar of the parish.
VIRGINIA. *[She crosses to him, shakes his hand]* Lady Canterville spoke of you. Please sit down.
VICAR. *[Sitting]* I've been away. London. A brief holiday.
VIRGINIA. Where is Mrs. Dampier?
VICAR. She'll pay her respects tomorrow. Wednesday is my wife's day for respects.
VIRGINIA. You're so formal in this part of the world. It's hard to get used to.
VICAR. I fear it's inbred. The people of this village are creatures of habit. *[Lightly]* How do you find Canterville Chase?
VIRGINIA. I'm enchanted by it. *[Moves in front of sofa]* You see, my sister and her husband have always wanted to live in England. Horace's business interests have done well enough that he can retire here at an early age. Naturally, I tagged along.
VICAR. You find nothing ... uh ... 'strange' about this place?
VIRGINIA *[Looks to portrait]* You're speaking of Sir Simon.
VICAR. Yes.
VIRGINIA. Sir Simon de Canterville has met his match in Horace Otis.
VICAR. Oh, dear. You mean there's been some 'unpleasantness'?

[HORACE followed by LUCY enters]

HORACE. Nothing we can't handle, Vicar. *[HORACE crosses D to VICAR and pumps his hand forcifully]* We Americans know how to handle ghosties and beasties and things that go bump in the night.

VICAR. *[Pulls back a mangled hand]* You have a strong grip, Mr. Otis.

HORACE. Comes from eating a good English breakfast. You've met Virginia.

VICAR. We were having a pleasant chat.

HORACE. My wife Lucy. *[VICAR starts to get up]*

LUCY. Stay seated, Vicar. So glad you dropped in. *[She sits VIRGINIA stands US of sofa]*

HORACE. We've heard a great deal about you.

VICAR. That's flattering.

LUCY. You run the orphanage.

VICAR. I never refer to it as an orphanage, Mrs. Otis. I call it — 'Children's Village'.

VIRGINIA. That's charming.

LUCY. And you run the home for old people, too.

VICAR. I never call it a home, Mr. Otis.

HORACE. What do you call it?

VICAR. 'Safe Harbor'. I encourage the residents to think of it as a hotel. That way they can check in when they wish and leave when they wish. Like guests.

HORACE. Must cost a pretty penny.

VICAR. *[Hesitantly]* Yes . . . a pretty penny.

LUCY. Virginia, ring for Mrs. Umney.

VICAR. I can't stay.

LUCY. One cup of tea before you leave?

VICAR. Another time. For now, I just wanted to stop by and bid you welcome. I'm delighted you're comfortable.

LUCY. It hasn't been easy sleeping here.

VICAR. You mean . . . Sir Simon?

HORACE. He's a noisy sort of pest.

VICAR. *[Tense]* Oh, Mr. Otis, you mustn't talk like that. No telling what he'll do.

HORACE. It's more a question of what I might do.

VICAR. You haven't antagonized him?

HORACE. No, but he's antagonized me.

LUCY. My husband permits nothing to interfere with a good
night's sleep.

VIRGINIA. The ghost gave us quite a start when he first appeared.

LUCY. Ran after my daughters with a sword.

HORACE. Made a vulgar display of himself. No class at all.
Shrieking and yelling.

LUCY. We soon put him in his place, however.

VICAR. A sword, you say? Tsk, tsk. I fear you don't grasp the
gravity of the situation. Sir Simon can be quite **malicious**.

HORACE. In my book he's a fraud and a fake.

LUCY. *[Points to rug]* He allows me to erase the blood stain
every night — only it's back the next morning.

VIRGINIA. And he's forever changing the color. One morning it's rose; the next it's purple.

HORACE. The old boy's color blind.

LUCY. Lady Canterville told us what he did to the Duchess of
Bolton.

HORACE.   Sir Simon is against good American horse sense.
You know what they say about horse sense, Vicar? It dwells
in a stable mind. *[He laughs]* The ghost isn't going to
scare us again. It's going to be the other way around.

[MRS. UMNEY enters]

MRS UMNEY. Lady Canterville's nephew just rang up.

VICAR. That would be Lord Cecil.

LUCY. What did he want?

MRS UMNEY. He said if it wouldn't be inconvenient, he'd
stop by for a moment.

LUCY. How nice.

VICAR. Mrs. Umney, I was trying to tell these charming people
that Sir Simon can be dangerous.

MRS UMNEY. Isn't easy, Vicar. Americans are rebels.

HORACE. Come on. What exactly can that pile of floating ectoplasm do?

MRS UMNEY. *[Steps DS]* Mrs. Biddy, the former housekeeper, woke up one morning and saw a skeleton seated in an armchair by the fire reading her diary.

VICAR. How very rude of the skeleton.

MRS UMNEY. Poor thing had to be confined to bed for six weeks.

LUCY. The skeleton?

MRS UMNEY. No, Mrs. Biddy.

VIRGINIA. Just too much imagination.

HORACE. Once you give in to Sir Simon's foolishness, you become a willing victim.

LUCY. He scattered my husband's papers all over the upstairs hall. *[MRS. UMNEY moves to the portrait]*

HORACE. A petulant thing to do. Immature.

MRS UMNEY. He's been acting unusually restless.

VIRGINIA. Especially for such an old spirit.

HORACE. Second night we were here, we heard him rattling all over the place in his suit of armor.

MRS UMNEY. That's how he frightens Jennie.

VICAR. What did you do?

HORACE. Do? What any sensible man would do.

VICAR. What **would** any sensible man do, Mr. Otis? What did you do?

HORACE. I said, 'Boo'.

VICAR. *[Incredulous]* Boo?

AMERICANS. Boo.

MRS UMNEY. I don't believe anyone has ever said 'Boo' to Sir Simon before.

LUCY. There's more.

VICAR. *[Worried]* I'm not sure I want to hear it.

LUCY. I knew we weren't going to get a wink if that charging kept up, so I offered him an oil can.

VICAR. Oil can!

VIRGINIA. It's what the girls use for their bikes.

LUCY. I said, 'My dear man, I must insist on your oiling
   that oversized tin can you're wearing.'
VICAR. *[Shocked]* You didn't!
LUCY. I did.
VICAR. What happened then?
LUCY. He fell over backwards and rolled down the stairs.
VIRGINIA. Woke the entire house.
VICAR. Mr. and Mrs. Otis — you're tempting fate.
HORACE. Not at all. I thought it would be wise for
   Sir Simon and me to know where we stood right off the
   bat.
VICAR. Off the bat? What on earth does that mean?
LUCY. It means that Sir Simon will either behave himself, or
   he'll have to go.
VICAR. Go! Go where? This is his home.
LUCY. Then it's time he started acting like it. His manners are
   worse than my daughters.
VIRGINIA. I feel the reason he made such a racket was be-
   cause he couldn't see in the dark.
HORACE. Virginia was very kind.
MRS UMNEY. She gave Simon a box of candies.
VIRGINIA. He seemed quite annoyed. Didn't even thank
   me.
VICAR. I'm afraid people from the colonies aren't what
   Sir Simon is accustomed to. I'm genuinely worried.
HORACE. We can take care of ourselves.
VICAR. I'm not worried about you. I'm worried about
   Sir Simon.
LUCY. Enough talk about the silly ghost. *[Shift in mood]*
   Vicar, I wonder, could we have a visit to Children's
   Village?
VICAR. *[Stands]* What better time than the present? I'm
   on my way there now. Do join me.
HORACE. Great idea.
LUCY. *[Remembers]* Oh, Lady Canterville's nephew.
VIRGINIA. I'll see him. Go along, both of you.

LUCY. Invite him for tea. The English can't seem to live without it.

VIRGINIA. I will.

HORACE. Come along, Lucy, Vicar. *[Inhales deeply]* Great day for a walk.

[HORACE marches into the garden]

LUCY. We're coming.

[LUCY exits after him]

VICAR. *[Stands]* Your brother-in-law and sister are 'confident' people, aren't they?

VIRGINIA. They don't let any grass grow under their feet.

VICAR. Grass grow under their feet? What a funny language you Americans speak. Poor Sir Simon . . . there'll be trouble . . . serious trouble . . . .

[VICAR exits into garden, shaking his head, mumbling]

MRS. UMNEY. The Vicar is upset.

VIRGINIA. Sir Simon is an upsetting influence. Go along and see if there's anything extra nice for tea.

MRS. UMNEY. Yes, Miss. *[MRS. UMNEY crosses DR. VIRGINIA moves to sofa, sits]* There is one thing . . . .

VIRGINIA. Yes?

MRS. UMNEY. Perhaps Madam Balaklava could help.

VIRGINIA. Who's Madam Balaklava?

MRS. UMNEY. A spirit medium, Miss Virginia. And a psychic researcher. Quite successful at ridding other estates of ghosts and ghouls.

VIRGINIA. You're not serious?

MRS. UMNEY. If you really want to get rid of Sir Simon, and I'm not sure I approve, Madam Balaklava is the only one who can help.

[PAM and WENDY, still dressed in jeans, come charging into the room from USC]

WENDY. Give it back! One of those is mine!

PAM. Not if I have them both!

WENDY. I'll get it back if I have to break your arm.

VIRGINIA. Get what back? You sound like a karate nut.

WENDY. She has my deodorant spray.

VIRGINIA. You girls ought to shape up. You do nothing but run in and out of every room. With all the clothes you have, I'll never understand your passion for jeans. You're too old for all this adolescent nonsense, anyway. *[Pause, then to MRS. UMNEY.]* You were saying something about a Madam Balaklava.

MRS. UMNEY. She's famous in these parts.

PAM. What for?

MRS. UMNEY. For one thing, she got rid of Martin the Maniac.

WENDY. *[Greatly impressed]* Who's he?

MRS. UMNEY. Sometimes he's known as 'The Masked Mystery'.

PAM. He sounds exciting.

MRS. UMNEY. He terrorized Milford Manor for centuries.

VIRGINIA. And this Madam Balaklava exorcised — is that what you're saying?

MRS. UMNEY. I don't know about that, Miss, but she certainly got rid of him. Not only that, she banished Hester the Horrid from Heathcliff House.

VIRGINIA. You're putting us on.

MRS. UMNEY. No, Miss. Madam Balaklava is a genius when it comes to the 'Unknown'.

WENDY. *[Fascinated]* If she's so great, why hasn't she been here before?

MRS. UMNEY. No one has requested her presence. She doesn't 'de-ghost' unless she's invited.

VIRGINIA. De-ghost? Lot of mumbo-jumbo. I can accept the presence of Sir Simon. In a way, I feel rather sorry for the poor man, but a ghost named Martin the Maniac,

and another called Hester the Horrid is going too far.
MRS. UMNEY. You don't want to forget Lady Joan the
  Graveless. *[VIRGINIA throws up her hands in despair]*
PAM. What was she famous for?
MRS. UMNEY. The popular press of the day referred to her
  as 'The Corpse-Snatcher of Chertsey Barn'. *[PAM and
  WENDY are mesmerized and barely suppress gasps]*
VIRGINIA. You're fortunate, Mrs. Umney, that Sir Simon
  has never done **you** any harm.
MRS. UMNEY. I am, indeed. Others haven't fared so well
  from family ghosts. A dear friend of mine was driven to
  the brink of despair, courtesy of The Vampire Duchess.
PAM. *[Bug-eyed]* Vampire Duchess! This is better than
  the late, late show.
MRS. UMNEY. Yes — the Duchess of Startup. Until Madam
  Balaklava visited the Startup Castle no one would come
  anywhere near the place.
VIRGINIA. As long as Sir Simon isn't too malicious, I see
  no need to send for a psychic researcher.
MRS. UMNEY . *[Shrugs]* As you wish, Miss.

[MRS. UMNEY exits DR]

WENDY. Virginia, don't you love all this stuff?
VIRGINIA. Stuff is right. Stuff 'n nonsense. I don't know
  why Mrs. Umney feels she has to keep us entertained with
  all these ghost stories. *[Soft laugh]* Martin the Maniac.
PAM. *[Stands]* Come on, Wendy.
WENDY. *[Stands]* I'm ready.
VIRGINIA. Ready for what?

[PAM moves into the garden, followed by WENDY]

PAM. You'll hear about it later.
VIRGINIA. *[Calls after them]* Women of mystery, aren't you?

[JENNIE enters]

JENNIE. The Duke of Cheshire, Miss Virginia.

[JENNIE exits. A good-looking young man, CECIL, enters UC, walks to VIRGINIA]

CECIL. Ah, Mrs. Otis. This is a pleasure. *[She holds out her hand. He takes it, shakes gently]*

VIRGINIA. I'm not Mrs. Otis. She's my sister.

CECIL. *[Releases her hand]* Then you're — ?

VIRGINIA. Virginia Washington.

CECIL. *[Smiling]* What could be more American than that? I hope I'm not intruding. I happened to be driving this way and thought I would call and introduce myself.

VIRGINIA. I'm glad you did. We wanted to meet you but my sister and her husband have gone with the Vicar. A tour of Children's Village.

CECIL. Wonderful place. *[Shakes his head]* Too bad, though.

VIRGINIA. Why do you say that, your Lordship?

CECIL. Call me Cecil. When people use the title, I feel like a prize snob. *[CECIL sees the portrait, crosses to it. VIRGINIA studies him]*

VIRGINIA. You didn't answer my question.

CECIL. Hmmmmm?

VIRGINIA. About Children's Village.

CECIL. *[Turns]* It's bankrupt. Hopelessly so. Same thing for Safe Harbor. The Vicar has a warm heart, but no business sense.

VIRGINIA I noticed his church seems a little the worse for wear.

CECIL. The roof leaks, the windows are cracked, and on a cold day the congregation shivers through its prayers. *[Back to portrait]* I trust he's being a gentleman.

VIRGINIA. I can't give you a good report about your kinsman.

CECIL. Sir Simon probably wants you out of the place. He
    never could abide strangers.
VIRGINIA. We'll be friends in no time.
CECIL. *[Smiles]* You and I, you mean?
VIRGINIA. *[Smiling also]* Sir Simon and myself.
CECIL. You've got spirit. I'll say that for you.
VIRGINIA. Let's forget about 'spirit'. *[Stands]* Cecil, I wonder
    do you know the meaning of the inscription on the land-
    ing?
CECIL. *[Faces her]* You mean what's on the stained glass
    window?
VIRGINIA. Yes *[Recites]*
        'When a golden girl can win
        Prayer from out the lips of sin,
        When the barren almond bears,
        And a little child gives away its tears –'
CECIL. *[Finishes]*
        'Then shall all the house be still
        And peace come to Canterville.'
VIRGINIA. It's painted in such curious letters, almost faded
    out. Took me a long time to decipher it all.
CECIL. Sorry I can't help you. I don't know what it means.
    Been there for centuries. Like the blood stain.
VIRGINIA. You will stay for tea.
CECIL. I'd be delighted.
VIRGINIA. Lucy and my brother-in-law will be back in plenty
    of time.
CECIL. *[Crosses C]* Then we have time for a walk. Why
    don't you show me the gardens?
VIRGINIA. Happy to.
CECIL. *[Crosses L]* I was hoping you'd say that. Remember,
    you must never say no to a relative of Sir Simon de
    Canterville. The old boy might take offense.
VIRGINIA. I make it a point never to offend a ghost.

[VIRGINIA crosses L, enters the garden. CECIL follows. As soon as he exits, stage darkens. Peal of thunder, sound of ancient clock striking the hour of four. Again – peal of thunder. SIR SIMON, in a rage, storms through the drapes]

SIR SIMON. 'Doom and gloom, thunder and spite! Curses on all who mock my might!' *[Looks around, disappointed]* Where is everyone? *[Another peal of thunder]*

[JENNIE enters UC, doesn't see the ghost at once]

JENNIE. Did you call out, Miss Virginia? *[She sees SIR SIMON, screams]*
SIR SIMON. I'll turn your hair white, my girlie! *[JENNIE runs behind the large chair, SIR SIMON in pursuit]*
JENNIE. Help, Mrs. Umney! Mrs. Umney! He's out of his room again! *[She runs for the servant's door]*
SIR SIMON. I'll rattle your bones when I catch you!
JENNIE. I'm giving notice!

[JENNIE exits – fast. SIR SIMON is DR. WEEDS enters through the French doors]

WEEDS. That you yellin', Jennie?
SIR SIMON. *[Turns menacingly, his hands as if to strangle]* No! It was me, and I'm going to plant you in your own garden, Mr. Weeds!
WEEDS. YIPES!

[WEEDS turns fast, runs into garden]

WEEDS. It's Sir Simon! Run for your lives!
SIR SIMON. *[Delighted with his mischief, SIR SIMON gives chase, stops C and does a jig-step – like a happy child]* I'll drive them out yet, I will, I will. *[He gives chase to*

WEEDS again. As he starts out, PAM hurries in. She's been doing her hair and has a can of hair set in her hand. She directs spray at SIR SIMON and hits him]

SIR SIMON. Ouch! *[He turns to confront PAM]* Beware!

PAM. Beware, yourself. You're one bad joke!

SIR SIMON. You dare call Sir Simon de Canterville one bad joke!

PAM. Believe me, I dare!

SIR SIMON. You'll regret this!

PAM. *[Mockingly]* You're going to scare yourself! *[SIR SIMON moves to grab her. PAM turns and quickly sprays him again]*

SIR SIMON. Stop it, stop it!

PAM. Who's afraid of the ghastly ghost!

SIR SIMON. Wretched female! *[He slaps at her, dancing about in an agitated state as she moves out of range]*

PAM. You great big grisly ghoul! Do you really want a fight? *[She advances menancingly with hair spray can]*

SIR SIMON. *[Arms up to protect himself]* No, No! *[PAM lightly sprays him. He turns to run into the garden]*

PAM. Come back! Fight like a Canterville!

[Just as SIR SIMON reaches the French doors, there is another peal of thunder, and a ghostly figure wearing a white sheet, looking like a Halloween goblin, hurries in, L, its arms waving spookily. Obviously WENDY in costume]

WENDY. Boo!

SIR SIMON. *[Terrified]* Aaaaauuuuugggggh!

[Quickly, SIR SIMON turns on his heel, runs across stage for the safety of the drapes. As he passes PAM she gets in another blast. At the drapes, SIR SIMON

turns back, livid] I will be avenged! *[PAM is laughing so
hard she has to sit down in the large chair]*
WENDY. Boo!

*[WENDY, arms outstretched under the sheet, runs for
the ghost. Alarmed, SIR SIMON flees behind the
sanctuary of the drapes. Peal of thunder on his
escape. Fast curtain]*

Scene 3

SCENE: A few nights later. French doors are closed.

[JENNIE is leading in MRS. DAMPIER]

JENNIE. Come right in, Mrs. Dampier.
MRS. DAMPIER. Thank you, Jennie. I hope Mr. and Mrs. Otis won't
be offended by my coming at this late hour. *[JENNIE indi-
cates sofa. MRS. DAMPIER sits]*
JENNIE. I don't think so, Ma'am. Y'see, they're not expecting
to get any sleep tonight.
MRS. DAMPIER. Why?
JENNIE. It's Madam Balaklava, Ma'am.
MRS. DAMPIER. The psychic?
JENNIE. Yes, Mr. Otis says he's had it with the ghost. Oh,
Sir Simon has been behaving something awful.
MRS. DAMPIER. I'm sorry to hear that.
JENNIE. He got into Weeds' greenhouse and broke a lot of
glass.
MRS. DAMPIER. I've never known Sir Simon to be so willful.
JENNIE. Even Mrs. Umney has turned against him. He ma-
terialized in the kitchen and poured flour over the floor.
And he turned her custard dessert sour.
MRS. DAMPIER. Shocking.

JENNIE. We think Madam Balaklava will set things right.

MRS. DAMPIER. I don't know what the Vicar is going to say about this. Augustus takes a dim view of mediums and psychics.

MRS. UMNEY. Mrs. Dampier! We didn't expect you tonight.

MRS. DAMPIER. Obviously, and I didn't expect to be here, but the Vicar has a nasty cold, so I'm taking on his duties.

MRS. UMNEY. Don't stand there like a stick, Jennie. Run along and fetch your mistress.

JENNIE. Right away, Mrs. Umney.

[JENNIE exits UC]

MRS. DAMPIER. What's this about Madam Balaklava coming here this evening?

MRS. UMNEY. If you could see and hear some of the things Sir Simon's been up to . . . .

MRS. DAMPIER. Jennie was telling me. Still, I don't see the necessity for summoning that dreadful Balaklava fraud to Canterville Chase.

MRS. UMNEY. There's no controlling the ghost. The girls say he's gone bananas.

MRS. DAMPIER. Bananas?

MRS. UMNEY. Forgive me. When one is around Americans, one is inclined to pick up their peculiar expressions.

MRS. DAMPIER. I was afraid there'd be trouble when I first heard The Chase was for sale.

MRS. UMNEY. Sir Simon's been generally disagreeab' Besides, he's tried to keep Lord Cecil and Virgini part. They belong together.

MRS. DAMPIER. How?

MRS. UMNEY. Every time Lord Cecil is about ay some- thing romantic, the ghost makes him have ent sneezing fit.

MRS. DAMPIER. How ungallant of Sir Si roast beef right

MRS. UMNEY. The other evening he too off the table and sent it sailing to th

MRS. DAMPIER. Good gracious.

MRS. UMNEY. It was stuck up there dripping gravy for almost two days. We had a frightful time getting it down. Finally, Weeds harpooned it with a pitchfork.

MRS. DAMPIER. Like living in a Chamber of Horrors.

MRS. UMNEY. So, Madam Balaklava was sent for.

MRS. DAMPIER. She's a charlatan.

MRS. UMNEY. She got rid of Martin the Maniac, Hester the Horrid, Lady Joan the Graveless —

MRS. DAMPIER. *[Holds up her hand in protest]* You're an impressionable woman, Mrs. Umney. Has anyone thought of speaking calmly and rationally to Sir Simon?

MRS. UMNEY. Won't do any good, speaking to the ghost. He's set in his ways.

[LUCY enters followed by VIRGINIA]

LUCY. What an unexpected pleasure.

MRS. DAMPIER. I hope this isn't an imposition.

VIRGINIA. *[Moves to large chair]* No indeed, we're all excited tonight.

MRS. DAMPIER. I wish you didn't feel it necessary to call on Madam Balaklava.

LUCY. *[Sits]* I'm afraid we have no choice.

VIRGINIA. At first we were quite willing to live and let live.

LUCY. Now we're afraid that unless the ghost is stopped, he may do serious injury. Has Mrs. Umney told you about the past?

MRS. DAMPIER. Most distressing. *[Then]* I'll come to the reason for my visit, if I may. We're having a church bazaar on.

MRS. UMNEY. To raise funds for Children's Village?

MRS. DAMPIER. And for Safe Harbor.

MRS. UMNEY. They can use the money. They owe everyone in the village.

LUCY. *[Stiff]* That'll be all, Mrs. Umney.

MRS. UMNEY. Yes, Madam.

[She exits DR]

LUCY. I don't know what we'd do without Mrs. Umney, but
   at times, she acts more like a member of the family than
   a housekeeper.
MRS. DAMPIER. I wouldn't let her get away. Quite difficult
   to find good servants these days.
VIRGINIA. We'll hang on to her.
MRS. DAMPIER. Is there something you might donate? All
   in a good cause.
LUCY. I'm sure we can think of something.

[PAM enters]

PAM. Dad's standing out on the steps waiting for that witch.
LUCY. Madam Balaklava is not a witch.
VIRGINIA. She's a psychic researcher.
PAM. Bet you're here about the bazaar, Mrs. Dampier.
MRS. DAMPIER. True.
LUCY. *[To PAM]* We'll have to think of something extra
   special to donate.
PAM. That's easy.
VIRGINIA. What do you suggest?
PAM. Why don't we donate Sir Simon's old suit of armor?
MRS. DAMPIER. *[Nervously]* His armor? Oh, dear.
LUCY. That's a marvelous suggestion.
PAM. And we can get a good night's sleep for a change. *[Crosses
   to the desk chair, sits]*
MRS. DAMPIER. But, Pamela, should we deprive Sir Simon of
   his armor?
PAM. Why not?
LUCY. It's yours with our blessing. I'm certain the Vicar will
   be pleased. Ought to bring a good price.

[JENNIE enters]

JENNIE. *[Excitedly]* Madam Balaklava has just driven up.
MRS. DAMPIER. *[Stands]* I don't want to see her. She's an awful bore. I'll leave now. *[Crosses DR]* Thank you for the armor. *[Peal of thunder]* Oh!

[MRS. DAMPIER hurries off]

PAM. Bet that thunder is Sir Simon acting up.
LUCY. See to the door, Jennie.
JENNIE. Yes, Ma'am.

[JENNIE exits UC as WENDY darts in]

WENDY. Has the seance started?
VIRGINIA. Tonight is not a seance. We're simply bidding a farewell to the ghost.
WENDY. *[Enraptured]* I bet Madam Balaklava will perform the exorcism with incense and incantations.
PAM. I'm going to question her about Martin the Maniac.
LUCY. Sorry to disappoint you two, but whatever Madam Balaklava does — will be done without your presence.
PAM and WENDY. What!
VIRGINIA. No telling what might happen.
PAM. You mean we're going to miss all the action?
VIRGINIA. This is a serious business. It's not supposed to be fun and games.
PAM. What a gyp!
WENDY. Please, can't we stay?
LUCY. Go on. Off to your rooms. Watch the B.B.C.
WENDY. Can't we at least have something to eat first?
LUCY. Of course. But please be quiet while Madam Balaklava is here.
WENDY. *[Moves DR]* Come on, Pam. *[Sighs]* What a life.
PAM. *[Follows after WENDY]* We should be in here with the ghost. It's definitely discrimination.

WENDY. I don't understand the older generation.

> *[PAM and WENDY exit. Offstage voices of HORACE
> and MADAM BALAKLAVA. LUCY and VIRGINIA
> turn USC]*

MADAM BALAKLAVA. The house positively reeks of ghostly
vibrations.
HORACE. That's not so surprising, considering Sir Simon is
always up to something.

> *[HORACE enters first, stands R, followed by MADAM
> .BALAKLAVA, an outrageous creature, heavily made-up,
> dressed colorfully and wearing enough junk jewelry
> to stock a small boutique. She's gushy, disorganized and
> obsessed with the 'occult']*

HORACE. Madam Balaklava, this is my wife, Lucy, and my sister-
in-law, Virginia.
LUCY. We're so pleased you could come.
MADAM BALAKLAVA. *[Moves to LUCY]* My poor woman,
how you must have suffered. Your husband has told me
of your terrible experiences with Sir Simon. *[Looks around,
wary]* Danger is in the air. *[The others exchange worried
glances]*
VIRGINIA. What kind of danger?
MADAM BALAKLAVA. *[Sees the blood stain, points dramati-
cally]* Aha!
ALL. What?
MADAM BALAKLAVA. *[Steps to spot]* The blood of Lady Eleanor
de Canterville.
VIRGINIA. They say she died of a broken heart.
MADAM BALAKLAVA. *[Studies the room. All watch in-
tently. She points UR]* Aha!
ALL. What?
MADAM BALAKLAVA. The draped room.
LUCY. It's all bricked up.

VIRGINIA. With bricks.

MADAM BALAKLAVA. *[Mysteriously]* Behind those drapes, the brothers of Lady Eleanor chained Sir Simon to the wall, with food and water just out of reach.

VIRGINIA. How awful.

MADAM BALAKLAVA. The crimes of Sir Simon were awful, too. Did you know he sacked the parish church?

HORACE. No!

MADAM BALAKLAVA. The very church that stands in Canterville Village today. Oh, Sir Simon was a terror.

HORACE. Still is.

MADAM BALAKLAVA. *[Conversational]* But Martin was fond of him.

HORACE . Martin?

MADAM BALAKLAVA. Martin the Maniac. I banished him from Milford Manor months ago.

HORACE. Is there anything special we should be doing?

MADAM BALAKLAVA. How do you mean?

LUCY. Preparing for Sir Simon's departure.

VIRGINIA. We've already made arrangements to sell his suit of armor.

[MRS. UMNEY enters]

MRS. UMNEY. Madam Balaklava. You must help these Americans, Madam. The ghost has been wicked.

MADAM BALAKLAVA. Never fear, Balaklava's here. *[A general in command of her troops]* Mr. and Mrs. Otis, if you sit together — *[Points to sofa]* — here. *[LUCY stands, crosses to sofa, sits. HORACE sits beside her]*

VIRGINIA. Where do you want me?

MADAM BALAKLAVA. *[Points]* By the French doors. If the spirit attempts to flee into the garden, you must stop him.

VIRGINIA. How?

MADAM BALAKLAVA. *[Melodramatic, 'enacts' what
    VIRGINIA must do]* First, you must thrust out your
    arm. *[Illustrates]* Then you must murmur a low moan.
    [Demonstrates] O-o-o-o-w . . . .
HORACE. Sounds like a cow in pain.
MADAM BALAKLAVA. *[Insulted]* Please!
HORACE. Sorry.
VIRGINIA. What else?
MADAM BALAKLAVA. If he attempts to run by you, say –
    'Away, away, you'll not escape this day. Turn back, I say
    and fade away.' Got that?
VIRGINIA. I feel ridiculous.
MADAM BALAKLAVA. I must insist.
VIRGINIA. *[Resigned]* Anything to help.
MADAM BALAKLAVA. I'm certain he won't even make for the
    garden. By the time I'm done with him, he'll be mist on the
    moors.
HORACE. *[Eager]* I'm ready.
LUCY. So am I.
MADAM BALAKLAVA. Lower the lights, Mrs. Umney.
    [MRS. UMNEY goes to some switch. Lights dim]
LUCY. I'm nervous.
MADAM BALAKLAVA. Silence! *[Moves to the large
    chair, sits, easing into a trance]* I'm drifting . . . drifting . . .
    drifting . . . *[Pause, then]* I see a spirit on the stairs.
HORACE. What's he wearing?
MADAM BALAKLAVA. It looks like a large soup can.
LUCY. That's Sir Simon.
MRS. UMNEY. He's in his suit of armor.
MADAM BALAKLAVA. Ssssssh.
ALL. Ssssssh.
MADAM BALAKLAVA. *[Fingers to her forehead, eyes shut
    tight]* Yes . . . yes, it is Sir Simon de Canterville. I can see
    his two beady eyes behind the visor of his helmet. Shame,
    shame on you, restless spirit.
VIRGINIA. Somehow, I don't feel right about all this.

MADAM BALAKLAVA. *[Ignores her]* When he materializes,
no one must cry out or provoke him, for only then can I
work the necessary power to banish him from Canterville
Chase — forever. *[Peal of thunder]* Ghost of Sir Simon
de Canterville, I order you to appear! *[Others look from
one to the other. Nothing]*
HORACE. Perhaps he's losing his hearing.
LUCY. He's very old.
MADAM BALAKLAVA. Sssssssh. *[Going deeper into her
'trance']* 'Baleful spirit, house a'haunting,
Cease! Desist your power flaunting.
Off! Be gone! At end of day.
Fie! Don't fly. **Forever stay.**'

MRS. UMNEY. *[Nervous]* No, no, Madam Balaklava. You've
got it backwards. It's 'Fie and fly. You **cannot** stay'.
MADAM BALAKLAVA. 'Pinch of pepper, pinch of salt,
Lock you from your secret vault.
Twig of almond, full in bloom,
Stay **forever** in this room.'
MRS. UMNEY. *[Shocked]* No, no, that's not right. It's,
'Banish ever from this room'.
MADAM BALAKLAVA. 'Never more these chambers roam.
Horrid spectre, leave this home.
Other ghosts from vale or hill,
Come all you to Canterville!'
[Thunder]
MRS. UMNEY. It's supposed to be — '**Never** come to Canterville'.
MADAM BALAKLAVA. *[Eyes open]* How was I?
MRS. UMNEY. You did everything backwards.
MADAM BALAKLAVA. *[Bewildered]* I did?
HORACE. You invited Sir Simon to stay.
LUCY. And all sorts of other ghosts.
MADAM BALAKLAVA. Other ghosts? That's absurd.

[Crash of thunder. All look toward French doors. MARTIN THE MANIAC, wearing a black mask, enters]

MARTIN. Who calls Martin the Maniac from his sleep?
  [VIRGINIA and LUCY gasp]
HORACE. *[To MADAM BALAKLAVA]* You've done it, for sure.
MADAM BALAKLAVA. *[Confused]* I don't understand how I
  got things twisted.

  [MRS. UMNEY screams, points to garden as HESTER THE HORRID enters]

HESTER. Who takes me from my rest? Beware, beware.
  [VIRGINIA moves by desk]
MADAM BALAKLAVA. It's Hester the Horrid. What's she
  doing here?
HORACE. You tell me!

  [LADY JOAN enters DR]

LADY JOAN. Why am I here? What is this place?
MRS. UMNEY. *[Alarmed]* Lady Joan the Graveless!
LUCY. *[Shaking]* Oh, Horace.
HORACE. *[Takes her in his arms]* You'd better do something
  in a hurry, Madam Balaklava, or I'll see they take away
  your license.
MADAM BALAKLAVA. You can't do that.
VIRGINIA. Why not?
MADAM BALAKLAVA. Because I don't have a license.

  [More thunder. MARTIN moves R as VAMPIRE DUCHESS, wearing a long cape, enters USC]

DUCHESS. Someone will pay for disturbing my slumber.
VIRGINIA . Who's she?
MRS. UMNEY. It's the Duchess of Startup. The one they call the
  vampire.

LUCY. Vampire!
HORACE. *[Exasperated]* All we need now is Sir Simon.

*[Thunder, SIR SIMON jumps out from behind the
drapes]*

SIR SIMON. You have your wish! *[Bounces C, performing his
    lively jig-step]* You thought you'd get rid of me, did you?
    I've got a trick or two up my sleeve. *[To MADAM BALA-
    KLAVA]* I made you say things backwards, and now I've
    got an army to help me keep my place in Canterville Chase.
    Ha, ha, ha. *[All the spirits laugh]*
LUCY. What are we going to do?
MADAM BALAKLAVA. I don't know what you're going to do,
    but I know what I'm going to do.
HORACE. What?
MADAM BALAKLAVA. I'm getting out of here!

*[MADAM BALAKLAVA bolts from the chair, runs out
    past the VAMPIRE DUCHESS. She is quickly followed
    by LUCY and HORACE. VIRGINIA runs into the
    garden. MRS. UMNEY exits DR]*

SIR SIMON. *[Gleeful]* Go git 'em!

*[Eager, MARTIN runs after MADAM BALAKLAVA. HESTER
    runs after VIRGINIA. VAMPIRE DUCHESS chases HORACE
    and LUCY. LADY JOAN goes after MRS. UMNEY. Screams,
    thunder]*

AD LIBS. Run, run! Get the police! Don't look back!
SIR SIMON. *[Surveys the now-empty room, delighted.
    To audience]* One English ghost can handle a houseful of
    Americans any day. *[Triumphant]* Sir Simon de
    Canterville has only begun to fight! *[Thunder]*

CURTAIN

END OF ACT I

ACT II

Scene 1

SCENE: Same as ACT I. It's a short time later.

AT RISE OF CURTAIN: SIR SIMON stands at the USC entry calling out:

SIR SIMON. Sir Simon de Canterville has only begun to fight! *[He rubs his hands together, joyfully, steps DS]* They have underestimated me, and they will pay.

[LADY JOAN enters DR]

LADY JOAN. I discovered two noisy girls in the kitchen.
SIR SIMON. That's Wendy and Pam.
LADY JOAN. I chased them into the lane. It was wonderful sport.
SIR SIMON. Splendid.
LADY JOAN. *[Crosses to sofa, sits]* It's fortunate for us Madam Balaklava is so bad at what she does.

[MARTIN enters laughing madly]

MARTIN. Oh, that was jolly fun, Sir Simon. We ran them into the main hallway, up the stairs, and into the bell tower.
SIR SIMON. With the bats. Do sit down, Martin, you look a bit fatigued.
MARTIN. I am winded. Not as young as I used to be. *[He sits in large chair]*
LADY JOAN. Alas, none of us are.
MARTIN. *[Chuckles]* Balaklava has met her match in you, Sir Simon.

39

LADY JOAN. Thought she was ridding The Chase of its resident ghost, and instead of that she's returned the rest of us to our haunting behavior.

[VAMPIRE DUCHESS enters]

DUCHESS. This is a drafty old place. Not enough tapestries in the upper chambers.

SIR SIMON. Haven't you been here·before, Vampire Duchess?

DUCHESS. Never. *[Steps in]* I'm not in the havit of leaving Startup Castle. At least, I wasn't until Madam Balaklava did her worst. That woman is a menace.
MARTIN. Sir Simon gave her a lesson.
DUCHESS. I understand you've been having troubles.
SIR SIMON. Americans. You wouldn't believe what I've had to put up with. Sit down, Duchess, sit down.
DUCHESS. *[Crosses to sofa, sits beside LADY JOAN]* I'm happy to say Startup Castle has never had any Americans about the place. They chew something called gum, I understand.
SIR SIMON. They're strange people.
MARTIN. Barbaric in their customs, eh?
SIR SIMON. Quite. They refuse to take an English ghost seriously.
LADY JOAN. Deplorable, really.
MARTIN. Not too sporting of them, eh?

[HESTER enters from garden]

HESTER. The gardens are lovely. I found a patch of deadly nightshade.
SIR SIMON. Make yourself comfortable, my dear. *[He gestures to the chair, HESTER sits]*
LADY JOAN. You were speaking of the colonials, Sir Simon.

SIR SIMON. The Americans, yes. As I said, they have no
    respect for a ghost, or a ghost's feelings. If I meet one
    in the hallway she is likely to hand me a can of lubri-
    cating oil for my suit of armor.
HESTER. Appalling.
LADY JOAN. Uncouth.
DUCHESS. Inconsiderate.
MARTIN. Rude, even.
SIR SIMON. You haven't heard the rest. They are plotting
    to donate my armor to a church bazaar. *[Ghosts are
    stunned]*
MARTIN. A scandal!
HESTER. An outrage!
SIR SIMON. Never, in a brilliant and uninterrupted career of
    four hundred years, have I been so grossly insulted, and
    inhumanely treated.
LADY JOAN. Ah, but I do believe they'll behave differently
    after tonight's adventure. *[HESTER, DUCHESS, MARTIN
    applaud the sentiment]*
MARTIN. Hear, hear.
SIR SIMON. I have been assaulted with hair spray. Ridiculed.
    Scoffed at. *[Hand to his head in a gesture of anguish]* Oh,
    the shame of it all.
MARTIN. Overdoing it a bit, aren't you old boy?
SIR SIMON. *[Ignores him]* When I think of the housemaids
    who went into hysterics when I merely grinned at them.
HESTER. I recall the beautiful Lady Stutfield, who was
    obliged to wear a black velvet band around her throat
    to hide the mark of five fingers burnt upon her white
    skin.
SIR SIMON. *[Recalls]* Hee. Hee.
LADY JOAN. You were a naughty boy, Sir Simon.
DUCHESS. Naughty, naughty.
SIR SIMON. *[Boyishly]* Well, I always did have an eye for
    the ladies.
HESTER. You, Sir Simon, are a ghost we can all look up to.

MARTIN. Especially, since the rest of us are sitting. *[He laughs. Others follow along. SIR SIMON frowns. MARTIN sees his disapproval]* Beg pardon. Didn't mean to make light of the situation.

SIR SIMON. This is a serious business.

MARTIN. Hear, hear.

SIR SIMON. *[Back to reminiscing]* How I vividly recollect the night in June I caused panic on the lawn by playing a game of croquet.

LADY JOAN. Is that so extraordinary?

HESTER. It is when you consider the fact Sir Simon played the game with his own bones. *[Ghosts applaud]*

DUCHESS. Remember the night Lord Pinch cheated at cards and was found choking in his room, with the Ace of Hearts halfway down his throat?

MARTIN. And he swore the Canterville Ghost made him swallow it.

HESTER. You are a true artist, Sir Simon.

SIR SIMON. If I say so myself — I have given celebrated performances.

DUCHESS. Perhaps you should adopt a new disguise. You were always rather good at them.

LADY JOAN. I know. You could appear to the Americans as Reckless Rupert, the Headless Earl.

ALL. Excellent idea. Splendid. Bravo. *[Ghosts applaud]*

SIR SIMON. That is an extremely difficult makeup. The preparation takes three hours. Besides, the boots don't fit me anymore, and I lost the pistol that goes with the belt.

HESTER. What a shame.

MARTIN. *[Gleefully recalling]* Don't forget the butler who shot himself in the pantry when he saw your green hand tapping at the window.

DUCHESS. He didn't shoot himself in the pantry. He shot himself in the big toe.

SIR SIMON. All my past achievement comes back to haunt

me. After all the glory, some wretched modern Americans
come here and mock my spirit.

LADY JOAN. Dear, dear, your nerves are quite shattered.

SIR SIMON. *[Burst of anger]*   I will have my revenge!

MARTIN. Lady Joan is correct.

SIR SIMON. There's nothing the matter with my nerves. It's
my pride that's suffering.

DUCHESS. Martin means the Americans. They'll behave more
sensibly after Madam Balaklava's fiasco.

SIR SIMON. I haven't told you the worst.

HESTER. There's more?

SIR SIMON. They're going to install television.

ALL. *[Shocked]* Television? *[Long pause, then]*

LADY JOAN. What's television?

SIR SIMON. I'm not quite sure, exactly. But from the way
they describe it, I gather it makes a great deal of noise
and never really says anything.

HESTER. How could you haunt with a thing like that in
the house?

MARTIN. It would destroy the mood.

LADY JOAN. You'll forbid it, of course.

SIR SIMON. I shall certainly make my opinions known.

MARTIN. Hear, hear. *[Stands]* You'll have to excuse
me now, Sir Simon. I must be on my way.

LADY JOAN. *[Stands]* So must I. I want to stop off at
the church graveyard and tell a few old friends I'm back
in town.

DUCHESS. *[Stands]* Always a pleasure, Sir Simon.

HESTER. *[Stands]* We must get together more often. We
only seem to see each other when Madam Balaklava is
messing about.

LADY JOAN. *[LADY JOAN and DUCHESS shake hands
with SIR SIMON]* Good night, Simon.

SIR SIMON. Good night, my dear. Thank you for coming.

[LADY JOAN exits via the garden]

DUCHESS. You're looking reasonably well, considering.
SIR SIMON. Kind of you to say so, Duchess. Adieu.

[DUCHESS moves to French doors, exits]

MARTIN. *[Slapping SIR SIMON on the shoulder]* You've
    got things under control, old boy. Chin up, stiff upper
    lip, what?
SIR SIMON. Good to see you again, you maniac.
MARTIN. If you don't mind, I'll go out the back way. Maybe
    there's a maid I might terrify.
SIR SIMON. Jennie's quite good at being terrified. Might give
    her a try.
MARTIN. *[Crosses DR]* I'll take your advice.
SIR SIMON. See you in a hundred years, or so.
MARTIN. *[Stops, turns back]* A hundred years? *[Laughs]*
    Ha, ha. You always were a jester, Sir Simon. A hundred
    years! A hundred years!
HESTER. You are an inspiration to us all. *[She moves to
    French doors]*
SIR SIMON. Thank you, Hester. I've always said you were
    horrid, but intelligent.
HESTER. Good night, ungentle spirit.

[HESTER and MARTIN exit]

SIR SIMON. *[Waves goodbye]* Good night. Fly carefully.
    [Voices from off–]
MADAM BALAKLAVA. Nothing like this has ever happened
    before!
HORACE. That doesn't help us much!
LUCY. What are we going to do now?

*[SIR SIMON hurries to the drapes, passes through. Few
seconds pass and then HORACE's head pokes into view
He cautiously surveys the room. Satisfied that it's safe,
he steps in. LUCY appears behind him]*

HORACE. Looks safe enough.
LUCY. You think they're gone?
HORACE Look for yourself. *[She does, moving behind sofa.]*

[MADAM BALAKLAVA hesitantly enters, looking right and left]

MADAM BALAKLAVA. It's Martin we have to be careful of. He's fond of throwing things.
HORACE. Not as fond as I am of throwing you out!
LUCY. Horace, please.
MADAM BALAKLAVA. *[Moves DS]* You're angry with me, Mr. Otis.
HORACE. How could you tell?
LUCY. You can hardly expect us to be pleased. We asked you here for the specific purpose of getting Sir Simon out of our hair.
HORACE. Instead of that, we found ourselves surrounded by a bunch of weirdo ghosts.
MADAM BALAKLAVA. Only Lady Joan is a weirdo. The others are merely eccentric.
HORACE. Ha!
MADAM BALAKLAVA. I shall return home and consult my cook book.
LUCY. Cook book?
MADAM BALAKLAVA. It's where I keep my incantation recipes. I'll solve this dilemma. Never fear, Madam Balaklava's here.
HORACE. I've heard that before. Just leave, Madam Balaklava.
LUCY. What about Sir Simon?
HORACE. We'll deal with him, ourselves. *[Scream from JENNIE, off]*
MADAM BALAKLAVA. Who's that?
LUCY. Sounded like Jennie.

[JENNIE hurries in from DR]

HORACE. It is.
JENNIE. Oh, oh. Horrible, horrible. That's what it was.
LUCY. *[Moves to JENNIE]* What's the ghost done now?
JENNIE. It wasn't our ghost. It was the one in the mask!
HORACE. *[Sarcastic]* The Lone Ranger?
LUCY. Horace, please. This is no joke.
MADAM BALAKLAVA. Obviously, the child is referring to
    Martin the Maniac, also known as the Masked Mystery.
HORACE. Jennie, you have my permission to show Madam
    Balaklava to the door.
JENNIE. What door?
HORACE. Any door! Only get her out of here before I
    make a spirit out of her.
JENNIE. Yes, sir. This way, Madam Balaklava.
MADAM BALAKLAVA. I'll think of something.
HORACE. *[Sticks his arm straight out]* Out!
MADAM BALAKLAVA. I can't understand it. *[Mumbling]*
        'Baleful spirit, house a 'haunting,
        Cease! Desist your power flaunting . . . .'

[She and JENNIE exit]

LUCY. What do you suppose went wrong?
HORACE. Sir Simon is much too clever for her. We're under-
    estimating the fellow.

[PAM and WENDY excited, enter from garden]

PAM. Wasn't it wonderful?
WENDY. We were chased half a mile at least.
HORACE. That's your idea of something wonderful!
WENDY. Wait 'til I write back home about this.
PAM. We saw Lady Joan float by.
WENDY. She looked lovely, like the heroine out of
    SON OF FRANKENSTEIN.

PAM. She didn't speak.
HORACE. Cut out that kind of talk. Gives my goosebumps gooseflesh.

[MRS. UMNEY enters UC]

MRS. UMNEY. Poor Madam Balaklava. She's in a wretched state. Her feelings have been hurt.
HORACE. *[Moves to large chair, sits]* How do you think we feel?
LUCY. You girls get to your rooms.
WENDY. What if there's more fun?
HORACE. If there is, we'll tell you in the morning.
PAM. *[Moves UC]* Let's go. *[WENDY follows]* I know! We can boobytrap the stairs with wire.

[PAM and WENDY exit]

MRS. UMNEY. Will you be wanting anything else, Mrs. Otis?
LUCY. I think we've had enough of everything for one evening.
MRS. UMNEY. In that case, good night.

[HORACE grunts. MRS UMNEY exits DR]

LUCY. I'll be happy when the girls leave for school.
HORACE. It will certainly calm down Canterville Chase.

[VIRGINIA enters through garden]

LUCY. How is Weeds doing?
VIRGINIA. He's threatening to resign.
HORACE. What now?
VIRGINIA. One of the spirits locked him in the potting shed after wetting him down with the garden hose. Poor man's shocked and shivering.

HORACE. *[Sighs, getting up]* I'll have a talk with him. If Sir Simon wants open warfare, that's what he's going to get.

   [Exits into garden]

LUCY. Madam Balaklava says there's nothing to fear from the other ghosts. They don't belong here, so they're not allowed to linger.
VIRGINIA. I wouldn't believe a thing she said. She couldn't read palms at a carnival for kangaroos.
LUCY. *[Sighs]* I suppose.
VIRGINIA. Why don't you go to bed. You look tired.
LUCY. I am. Very tired. *[Starts UC]*
VIRGINIA. *[Crosses to desk]* I think I'll stay up for a while. I have a few letters to write.
LUCY. *[Turns, smiles]* Are you hoping Cecil will call?
VIRGINIA. *[Grins]* Maybe.
LUCY. He's charming, and Lady Canterville is fond of you.
VIRGINIA. I don't need a matchmaker. Go along.
LUCY. Good night.

   [LUCY exits. VIRGINIA sits, takes pen and paper. Thunder. Stage lighting flickers. Startled, VIRGINIA looks around, then she becomes angry]

VIRGINIA. *[Stands]* Really, Sir Simon! Your behavior is extremely childish.
SIR SIMON. *[From behind the drapes]* Beware, beware !!!
VIRGINIA. *[Moves C, eyes on the drapes]* You're a silly old thing.

   [Infuriated, SIR SIMON leaps from behind the drapes]

SIR SIMON. Silly old thing? Auuuuuugh! *[Wears a cape, flopping hat with a feather. Also, he holds a broom, business end up in the air]*

Now I am going to terrify you! *[He lifts the broom as if he were about to decapitate some unfortunate in the Tower of London]*

VIRGINIA. Please be careful with that broom. If you break anything, my sister will be terribly upset.

SIR SIMON. I hear your pleas for mercy, but I am heartless!

VIRGINIA. *[Crosses to large chair, sits]* If you're planning to clank around all night, I suggest you do it in the cellar dungeon. You're becoming an awful bore in that rusty suit of armor.

SIR SIMON. I am merciless! Your fate is sealed. Your tears have no effect on me.

VIRGINIA. Tears? What tears? You don't think for one moment, I take you seriously?

SIR SIMON. *[Crushed]* Don't you?

VIRGINIA. When I was told the place had a resident ghost, I was charmed. But I wasn't told the resident ghost was also a pest and a nuisance.

SIR SIMON. A pest? You dare call Sir Simon de Canterville a pest?

VIRGINIA. I could call you a great many things, but I think 'pest' says it all.

SIR SIMON. You're supposed to be shaking in fear.

VIRGINIA. I'm sensible. I have no intention of shaking. Truth of the matter is — I'm sorry for you.

SIR SIMON. Sorry?

VIRGINIA. In much the same way I'd be sorry for a child who throws tantrums to get attention. Now take off that silly hat with the feather.

SIR SIMON. *[Takes it off, holds it in his hand]* I thought it had a nice touch.

VIRGINIA. *[Disapproves]* Dressing up in costumes just to be noticed, bringing your friends here uninvited.

SIR SIMON. I **invited** Lady Joan and the others.

VIRGINIA. Yes, but this doesn't belong to you anymore. *[Direct, reasonable]* I realize that you, as a ghost, have

certain unalienable rights. At the same time, you must
realize that we, living here, have rights, too. The girls
have been giving you a bad time. But they're off to
school soon, so no one will trouble you — if you behave.

SIR SIMON. Behave?! I must rattle my chains and groan
through keyholes. It is my only reason for existing.

VIRGINIA. That's no reason at all for existing. I must
say breaking your wife's heart was shameful.

SIR SIMON. How did I know she was going to suffer a
broken heart? *[Pouts]* Anyway, I don't think it was fair
of her brothers to starve me to death.

VIRGINIA. I could fix you a sandwich.

SIR SIMON. I don't want a sandwich! I want respect!

VIRGINIA. There's no need to shout.

SIR SIMON. Forgive me. It's been a trying night. May I
sit down? *[VIRGINIA nods. He sits]* You are much
nicer than the rest of your rude, vulgar and dishonest
family.

VIRGINIA. *[Stands, indignant]* It is you who are rude,
vulgar and dishonest. You think I don't know who keeps
stealing tubes of color from my paint box? *[Points to
rug]* Look at that spot. Who ever heard of emerald
green blood?

SIR SIMON. What do you expect me to do? It's difficult
to get real blood these days. As for the color, that's
entirely a matter of taste. The Cantervilles have blue
blood, for instance. I know you Americans don't care for
things like that.

VIRGINIA. Stick to the subject. You feel we have behaved
badly toward you.

SIR SIMON. *[Pouts]* You have.

VIRGINIA. We feel you have behaved badly toward us.

SIR SIMON. Bah.

VIRGINIA. We're not going to get anywhere always at each
others' throats.

SIR SIMON. *[Brightens]* Speaking of throats, did you hear

what I did to lady Stutfield? *[Hands to his own throat]*
She had to wear a band around her throat to hide the
mark of five fingers –

VIRGINIA. *[Cuts him off]* We must reach a compromise. If
you'll confine your ghostly goings-on to certain hours of
the night, and in authorized parts of the house, I assure you,
you will be treated with dignity.

SIR SIMON. And if I refuse?

VIRGINIA. Horace might find some way to ship you to
America. He's clever,you know.

SIR SIMON. *[Grimaces]* America!

VIRGINIA. Yes – you'd be quite a curiosity there.

SIR SIMON. *[Aghast]* Curiosity!

VIRGINIA. If that doesn't work, I imagine Madam Balaklava
can figure some new way to exorcise you. You're something of a challenge to her now.

SIR SIMON. *[Stands, fearful]* No! You must never let her
come back.

VIRGINIA. Ah, then you are afraid of what she can do.
[Pause] Sir Simon, we are not leaving.

SIR SIMON. Nor am I.

VIRGINIA. What's it to be, then – compromise or catastrophe?

SIR SIMON. You're an intelligent girl.

VIRGINIA. Then you agree?

SIR SIMON. *[Thinks]* Hmmmmm . . . on one condition.

VIRGINIA. Which is?

SIR SIMON. You make me that sandwich. *[He smiles]*

VIRGINIA. *[Smiles in return]* I'd be honored. *[Rises,
moves across stage]* I imagine after four hundred years
you've worked up quite an appetite.

SIR SIMON. *[Calls after her]* With good English mustard!
[He moves to follow. Curtain falls]

Scene 2

SCENE: The Same. One week later, in the afternoon.
PAM is standing at French doors, looking into the garden.
MRS. UMNEY enters DR with a suitcase. Ad Lib conver-
sation from the garden − sound of people laughing, talking.

MRS. UMNEY. I think this is what you wanted, Miss Pamela.
PAM. *[Turns]*   All my jeans go in that suitcase.
MRS. UMNEY. You'll have to wear a uniform at boarding
school, not jeans.
PAM. Ugh. A uniform. No way.
MRS. UMNEY. *[Moves UC]*   Boarding school is a privilege,
you'll enjoy it.

*[WENDY enters from garden in time to overhear
this last remark]*

WENDY. Maybe Pam'll enjoy it, but I won't. No boys!
MRS. UMNEY. *[Mildly shocked]* I'll put this in your room
with your other luggage. Weeds will fetch your trunk this
evening.

[She exits]

PAM. Thanks Mrs. Umney. *[To WENDY]* How's the bazaar
going?
WENDY. *[Crosses to sofa]* Everybody seems to be having
a good time.
PAM. I think it was nice of Mom and Dad to have it here on
the grounds.
WENDY. Mom and Dad are nice people. The Vicar is sure
busy, running from booth to booth, greeting everyone.

*[LUCY enters from DR, followed by JENNIE, who
carries a tray of small wrapped 'gifts']*

LUCY. Jennie, take the tray out to the pitch-penny stall. See
    if they'll need any more. *[To girls]* Are you packed?
WENDY. *[Frowns]* Almost. Weeds is bringing up the big
    trunk later.
LUCY. You can make yourselves useful. *[Takes the tray from
    JENNIE, hands it to WENDY]* See that Mrs. Midwinter
    gets this. *[WENDY takes the tray, moves toward PAM]*
PAM. We will.

    [They exit]

JENNIE. I think they're a bit unhappy, Ma'am.
LUCY. Because they're off to school?
JENNIE. I think they'd rather stay here.
LUCY. Not many girls would be enthusiastic about boarding
    school. They're used to the activity of a public high and
    the freedom.
JENNIE. They're disappointed in the ghost, too. He's been
    quiet as a mouse.
LUCY. Let's be grateful. I hope the Vicar does well.
JENNIE. Mrs. Umney and all the other ladies say it would be
    a tragedy if Reverend Dampier had to close down his charities.
LUCY. The Vicar has a large heart, but a small bank balance.
JENNIE. I heard your husband say it would also take a small
    fortune to save them.
LUCY. *[Looks L]* Shouldn't talk like that, Jennie. It's
    telling tales out of school. Hello, Reverend Dampier.

    [VICAR enters from garden, crosses to LUCY]

VICAR. Ah, Mrs. Otis. Everything is going splendidly.
    When people heard the bazaar was going to be held on
    the grounds of Canterville Chase, they flocked in. I can't
    thank you enough.
LUCY. It's the least we could do.
VICAR. The girls told me Sir Simon has been the model of a

gentleman recently. Excellent news.

JENNIE. Hard to understand, Vicar. Don't know what's
come over the ghost.

VICAR. Must be difficult for a spirit these days. People have
so many other things on their minds.

JENNIE. Took him a while to get used to foreigners, I suspect.
[LUCY stiffens] No offense, Ma'am.

LUCY. 'Newcomers', Jennie, has a much softer sound.

VICAR. I'm delighted you and your husband picked our village
for your home. We need new blood.

JENNIE. *[Points to rug]* That's another thing. Sir Simon has
let the spot almost fade away.

LUCY. At least the color doesn't keep changing.

*[MRS. DAMPIER, wearing a 'garden party' hat, enters
from garden, WEEDS behind her]*

MRS. DAMPIER. We'll need your help at the weight guessing
booth, Mrs. Otis.

LUCY. Right away.

MRS. DAMPIER. Weeds says Sir Simon's suit of armor will
take two men to lift.

LUCY. *[To WEEDS]* I'll tell my husband.

MRS. DAMPIER. I believe we'll make several hundred dollars.

LUCY. Wonderful.

*[The women exit. WEEDS takes some envelope from
his pocket]*

WEEDS. This came for you, Vicar. Hand-delivered. *[WEEDS
crosses to him]*

VICAR. *[Takes the letter, reads return address]* Oh, my. It's
from the bank.

WEEDS. Anything wrong?

VICAR. *[Worried]* I shouldn't think so. *[Lies]* The bank
is probably making a donation to the bazaar.

WEEDS. People is saying the bank is going to foreclose on
   you.
VICAR. Pay them no mind. Trust in Providence.
WEEDS. Whatever you say, Vicar.

   [WEEDS crosses DR and exits]

VICAR. *[Waits until he's gone and, then, nervous, he opens
   the letter, reads. Aloud to himself]* Oh, dear, dear, dear.
   [He sits in the large chair with a sigh]

   [VIRGINIA and CECIL enter from the garden]

CECIL. The weather couldn't be more perfect.
VIRGINIA. It's lovely. *[Sees VICAR]* Getting away from
   the crowd, Reverend? *[Moves C. CECIL moves DL]*
VICAR. I popped in to congratulate your mother on our
   success.
CECIL. Things do seem to be going well.
VICAR. *[Holds out the letter]* Not well enough, I'm afraid.
CECIL. *[Starts to sneeze]* I'm going to sneeze . . . ah . . . ah
   ah . . .ah . . .
VIRGINIA. *[Looks to drapes]* Remember our agreement,
   Sir Simon. *[Instantly, CECIL's sneeze subsides]*
CECIL. That's a relief.
VIRGINIA. *[Concerned]* What is it? *[Takes letter, reads]*
   'Dear Reverend Dampier, much as it grieves us here at the
   bank, we have no alternative but to begin legal action to
   take possession of the properties now know as Children's
   Village and Safe Harbor . . .'
CECIL. *[Distressed]* Surely, there's something that can be
   done.
VIRGINIA. *[Continues reading]* ' . . . unless we hear from
   you within 24 hours on plans to remedy the outstanding
   debts, we will commence action. We regret the unpleasantness and hope you will settle the account.'

CECIL. The letter is almost rude.

VIRGINIA. It's signed, 'Lord Orville Beaverpaddle.'

CECIL. I shall have a few choice words with Lord Beaverpaddle.

VICAR. He has every reason to be annoyed with me. He's
    extended the loan several times. I've put him off, hoping some-
    thing would turn up. Banks aren't in the business of losing money.
    The truth is both the Village and the Harbor are bankrupt.
    They have been for some time.

VIRGINIA. You're speaking in terms of money alone. But what
    about those old people who have their independence, and the
    children?

VICAR. *[Forces a smile]* We mustn't tell the others yet. It would
    ruin the bazaar. *[He stands, takes back the letter]* If you'll
    excuse me.

    [He exits into garden]

VIRGINIA. The bank won't foreclose. They can't. It would be
    inhuman.

CECIL. I wouldn't be so optimistic.

VIRGINIA. There's no point in being negative. That's too easy.
    *[Thunder. Sound of rain. Ad lib reactions of GUESTS, off-left.
    They turn to the garden]*

CECIL. What's happened to our beautiful weather?

VIRGINIA. The sun's all in shadow.

CECIL. Only a shower. It'll pass.

VIRGINIA. I hope so. First the letter from the bank and now rain.
    I'm afraid this isn't the Vicar's lucky day.

CECIL. I'd better see if I can help out. A lot of the tables are un-
    covered.

    [He starts for the French doors, is stopped by LUCY'S entrance]

LUCY. What a pity. Some of the guests are running for the green-
    house and — others are huddled under the trees.

MRS DAMPIER. *[From offstage]* Come along, this way, this way.

[She darts in from the garden, followed by two ladies, also wearing 'garden party hats.' They are MRS MUSGRAVE, who carries a pie, and MRS MIDWINTER]

MRS MUSGRAVE. Oh, Lord Cecil, I wonder if you could give Mr. Otis and the Vicar some help?
MRS MIDWINTER. They're folding down the striped umbrellas.
CECIL. To the rescue.

[He exits into the garden]

MRS MUSGRAVE. *[Holds up the pie]* I saved the raffle meringue. I'll put it here. *[She puts it on the desk]*
LUCY. *[Moves C]* Everyone, please. Sit down. The rain can't last. *[MRS MIDWINTER crosses to the sofa, sits. MRS DAMPIER sits in the large chair. MRS MUSGRAVE sits DL. VIRGINIA sits beside MRS MIDWINTER.]*
VIRGINIA. What bad luck.
MRS MUSGRAVE. *[Looks around the room]* I wonder if 'he' had anything to do with this?
MRS MIDWINTER. Who?
MRS MUSGRAVE. Sir Simon.
VIRGINIA. I can assure you, Sir Simon did not cause the rian.
MRS MIDWINTER. It's the sort of trick he's noted for.
MRS MUSGRAVE. Once, he ruined a garden party for Lord Cecil's mother.
LUCY. How?
MRS MIDWINTER. He waited until the guests were on the far side of the lawn, and then he caused thunder and lightning.
VIRGINIA. I don't see how you can hold Sir Simon accountable for that.
MRS MIDWINTER. This was the only place it happened. Sunshine everywhere else in the village.
MRS MUSGRAVE. Sir Simon, no doubt about it.

LUCY. We don't have problems with the ghost anymore.
MRS DAMPIER. Is that because of Madam Balaklava?
VIRGINIA. Please don't mention her name. It upsets Sir Simon.
MRS DAMPIER. You've become rather protective toward him.
LUCY. Virginia has grown fond of him. That's true.

[MRS UMNEY enters UC]

MRS UMNEY. Beg pardon, Mrs. Otis. Someone to see you. She
    says it's quite important.
LUCY. Who is it?
MRS UMNEY. It's Madam Balaklava.
VIRGINIA. *[Stands, alarmed]* Oh!
LUCY. I suppose I must see her.
VIRGINIA. No!
LUCY. What's the matter with you, Virginia? *[To MRS UMNEY]*
    Show her in.
MRS UMNEY. Yes, Ma'am.

[She exits UC]

VIRGINIA. Lucy, you mustn't see her. She mustn't stay.
LUCY. I've never seen you act like this.
MRS MUSGRAVE. I've never met a psychic researcher.
MRS MIDWINTER. They're much like anyone else, I imagine. Only
    different.

[MADAM BALAKLAVA dashes in, excited]

MADAM BALAKLAVA. Wonderful news, Mrs. Otis. Not only have
    I discovered where Sir Simon caused me to go wrong, but I know
    why he was able to do it.
LUCY. Tell me.
MADAM BALAKLAVA. I should have remembered — with an un-
    familiar house it requires a minimum of **two** visits before my
    powers are effective.

VIRGINIA. You must leave immediately.
MRS DAMPIER. Why must she leave?
VIRGINIA. Because . . . because I promised someone.
MRS MUSGRAVE. Promised someone what?
VIRGINIA. That Madam Balaklava would never come here again.
MADAM BALAKLAVA. You're upset, Virginia. But your worries
    are over. *[An announcement, stepping DS]* If everyone will
    remain perfectly quiet, I shall rid Canterville Chase of Sir Simon
    in a matter of seconds.
MRS MUSGRAVE. How thrilling!
MRS MIDWINTER. An unexpected treat!
MRS DAMPIER. *[To VIRGINIA]* Let her do it. It's the only way to
    get rid of her.
VIRGINIA. Madam Balaklava, please go!
    *[MADAM BALAKLAVA ignores her. Puts her hands to her forehead,
    incants. ALL lean forward, fascinated. Alarmed for fear of what Sir
    Simon might do, VIRGINIA moves to the drapes.]*
MADAM BALAKLAVA.
                    'Baleful spirit, house a'haunting,
                    Cease! Desist your power flaunting.
                    Off! Be gone! At end of day.
                    Fie and fly. YOU CANNOT STAY!'

*[Thunder. In a new rage, SIR SIMON zooms out of his walled room.
ALL stifle screams]*

SIR SIMON. *[To MADAM BALAKLAVA]* I warned you!
MRS MUSGRAVE. *[Stands, points]* There he is!
VIRGINIA. Sir Simon, let me handle this.
MADAM BALAKLAVA. I stand my ground! Strong as a psychic
    researcher and strong as Balaklava! Charge!
MRS DAMPIER. *[Runs into garden]* I'll get the Vicar.
MADAM BALAKLAVA. *[On with the exorcism]*
                    'Pinch of pepper, pinch of salt,
                    Lock you from your secret vault . . . '
SIR SIMON. STOP IT!

LUCY. *[Runs after MRS DAMPIER]* Horace, Horace! He's mis-
behaving again!
MADAM BALAKLAVA.
          'Twig of almond, full in bloom,
          Banish ever from this room . . . '
SIR SIMON. YOUR FATE IS SEALED!
MRS MUSGRAVE. He's dangerous.
MRS MIDWINTER. No telling what he might do. Come on.

*[MRS MIDWINTER flees out, MRS MUSGRAVE trails after her,
casting worried glances at the ghost. MADAM BALAKLAVA
continues on. SIR SIMON, furious, stomps his foot.]*

SIR SIMON. Out of this house. Out, out, **out**! Or I'll charge!
MADAM BALAKLAVA.
          'Never more these chambers roam.
          Horrid spectre, leave this home . . . '
*[SIR SIMON sees the pie on the desk, crosses to it, picks it up
and crosses DS to MADAM BALAKLAVA, who continues on in
her trance-like state.]*
MADAM BALAKLAVA.
          ' Other ghosts from vale or hill,
          Never come to Canterville!'
*[On 'Canterville' SIR SIMON smacks her square in the face with
the pie. SEE PRODUCTION NOTES]*
Eeeeeeek!
*[She stands in shock for a moment. VIRGINIA covers her mouth
to supress a shocked gasp. Quickly, MADAM BALAKLAVA re-
covers her dignity.]*
Good day, Virginia.
[She glares at SIR SIMON]
I have only one thing to say to you, Sir Simon.

*[She sticks out her tongue and gives him a raspberry. Then,
with considerable poise, her face dripping meringue, she exits
like royalty]*

SIR SIMON. *[Slaps his hands together]* So much for that old witch.

VIRGINIA. I'm disappointed in you

SIR SIMON. *[Moves to large chair, sits]* What have I done?

VIRGINIA. *[Moves DS]* Don't play the innocent.

SIR SIMON. Why should you be upset if I ran off that – *[Distastefully]* 'Psychic researcher.' Besides, you promised she'd never return.

VIRGINIA. She came here uninvited. It had nothing to do with me, and you know it. I'm talking about the weather. You darkened the skies, didn't you? You did it deliberately, and you even tried to make Cecil have another sneezing fit.

SIR SIMON. What if I did? I have to have fun, don't I?

VIRGINIA. I though we struck a bargain to respect one another. What people say about you is true. You're completely selfish.

SIR SIMON. *[Hurt]* I don't like it when you're angry with me. I got bored.

VIRGINIA. You make that sound like an excuse for anything. I am not going to stay and listen to you. *[She starts UC]*

SIR SIMON. I am so lonely and unhappy. Please don't go.

VIRGINIA. *[Turns]* Is this another of your tricks?

SIR SIMON. I really don't know what to do. I want to sleep and I cannot.

VIRGINIA. I'll fix you a glass of warm milk.

SIR SIMON. You don't understand. I haven't slept in over four hundred years. Forgive me for spoiling the bazaar. I can't bear to see other people happy when I'm so miserable.

VIRGINIA. There's no place where you can find rest?

SIR SIMON. *[Dreamily]* Yes . . . beyond the garden, beyond the pine-woods. The grass grows long and deep. The nightingales sing all night long.

VIRGINIA. *[Understands]* You mean – not of this earth?

SIR SIMON. I've been so wicked in my life, I'm not allowed to cross over. If only I could. To have no yesterday, no tomorrow, to forget time, to be at peace.

VIRGINIA. I wish I could help you.

SIR SIMON. You can. You know the prophecy on the window?

VIRGINIA. I don't know what the words mean.

SIR SIMON. You have a golden heart, you're good. The words mean . . .
that you must weep with me for my sins, because I have no tears,
and pray with me for my soul, because I have no faith. Would you,
Miss Virginia?

VIRGINIA. *[A bit frightened]* I'm not sure I understand.

SIR SIMON. *[Stands]* Come with me.

VIRGINIA. *[Reacts]* Where? Is it . . . dangerous?

SIR SIMON. You're my only hope. Wicked voices will whisper in
your ear, but the voices will not harm you, for against the courage
of a good heart, they are powerless. If you're afraid to come and
plead my case — I am forever doomed to dwell within these walls.

VIRGINIA. Poor ghost.

SIR SIMON. Will you help?

VIRGINIA. I'll do whatever I can.

SIR SIMON. And not be afraid?

VIRGINIA. *[She's afraid, but she forces herself to smile]* I'll try not
to be.

SIR SIMON. You will see fearful shapes in the darkness.

VIRGINIA. How . . . how do we begin?

SIR SIMON. *[He crosses to the French doors, looks into the garden]*
By passing beneath the almond tree. I am so weary of being wicked.

*[Thunder. He exits into the garden. Another peal of thunder.
VIRGINIA, apprehensive, stares after him.]*

VIRGINIA. *[Convincing herself]* I am not afraid.

*[She moves to follow the ghost on his strange journey. Just as
she passes through the French doors, another peal of thunder.]*

[JENNIE and WEEDS, cautious, enter from DR]

JENNIE. Look! There he is.

WEEDS. Miss Virginia's with him. You're lucky I'm here to protect
you, Jennie. *[They cross C, staring off-left]*

JENNIE. They're walking into the mist. I can barely make them out.
[JENNIE and WEEDS are shaking]
WEEDS. I wonder if she'll ever come back. I wonder if he'll let her?
JENNIE. Don't say that. Do something.
WEEDS. Don't worry, I'll rescue her. I'm brave.
JENNIE. *[Points into the garden]* They're disappearing.
WEEDS. Keep calm. I'm here.
JENNIE. Sir Simon's gone up in a puff of fog. Miss Virginia's gone,
too. I'm so scared I might faint.
WEEDS. I'll catch you. *[At which point WEEDS faints from sheer
terror]*
JENNIE. What did you go and do that for? Oh, oh. *[She runs out the
French doors.]* Come back, Miss Virginia! Come back!
WEEDS. *[Lifts his head from the floor, manages a feeble —]* Help.
[He faints again. Fast curtain]

Scene 3

SCENE: Same.   Early the next morning.   LUCY is
stretched out on the sofa, sobbing. MRS UMNEY comes from
DR with a cold cloth in a basin.

LUCY. My poor sister. Poor Virginia.
MRS UMNEY. There, there, Mrs. Otis. They'll find her.
LUCY. Where could the ghost have taken her? *[MRS UMNEY puts
the basin on the table, R, wrings cloth out]* He's never left the
grounds before.
MRS UMNEY. Miss Virginia is a sensible young woman. She can take
care of herself.
LUCY. I wish I could believe that.
MRS UMNEY. Here we go. A nice cold compress. It'll help you
relax.
LUCY. *[Sits up]* I don't want to relax. I want my sister back.

[JENNIE comes in. MRS UMNEY puts the compress back in the basin]

JENNIE. I've searched every room again. They haven't come back. They're not hiding anywhere.

LUCY. Jennie, you're absolutely sure of what you saw?

JENNIE. Yes, Ma'am. They disappeared into the drizzle. I ran after them, calling for Miss Virginia to come back, but I was too late.

[PAM and WENDY enter from the garden]

PAM. The sun's up now. Maybe that'll help them find Virginia.

WENDY. We've been up and down the lane, yelling for her.

[WENDY moves to DL chair, PAM to UL chair. They sit]

MRS UMNEY. In over four hundred years, Sir Simon has never been known to indulge in kidnapping. It's not his style.

JENNIE. He didn't seem to be kidnapping her, Mrs. Umney. She seemed to be going with him willingly.

MRS UMNEY. Talk sense, you silly girl.

[WEEDS enters DR]

LUCY. Where have you been?

JENNIE. *[Critical]* Probably fainting somewhere.

WEEDS. Hadn't ought to talk like that, Jennie. I had me a dizzy spell, that was all.

LUCY. Never mind all that. Where have you searched?

WEEDS. We went down by the gypsy camp.

MRS UMNEY. You don't think Sir Simon tried to sell her, so they could train her as a fortune teller?

LUCY. Oh, oh, oh. My baby sister! A fortune teller — with gypsies!

PAM. Wouldn't the gypsies be afraid?

WEEDS. Not of a spirit. They know all about such things.

WENDY. What did you find in the camp?

WEEDS. Nothing. But I got me palm read.

MRS UMNEY. You're no help, whatsoever.

JENNIE. Sir Simon had been acting so good.

WENDY. What about the pie in Madam Balaklava's face?

LUCY. Something's upset him, something's causing him to act this way. Why did he suddenly become restless again?

[HORACE enters from garden]

HORACE. I've never walked so long and so far in my life.

LUCY. You've brought her back?

HORACE. No. *[Communal groan]* I've been to the police. They're annoyed with Sir Simon, but they don't see how they could arrest him.

LUCY. Why not?

HORACE. Seems there's no precedent. They have no experience in arresting a ghost.

WEEDS. Maybe Scotland Yard could help.

HORACE. The constable has a call in for London. The minute he gets an okay, he'll issue a warrant.

LUCY. A warrant? For a ghost? What good will that do? Horace, you've gone as mad as the rest.

MRS UMNEY. Perhaps Madam Balaklava could help. *[Others react – she's apologetic]* Sorry.

[LADY CANTERVILLE enters UC with CECIL]

LADY CANTERVILLE. No one answered the door. I feel somewhat guilty, but I did warn you about Sir Simon.

HORACE. You didn't say he was likely to kidnap my sister-in-law.

CECIL. Old boy has never done anything like this before.

[NOTE: At this point, positions should be as follows: WEEDS, DR, MRS UMNEY by the sideboard. LUCY and LADY CANTERVILLE on the sofa. CECIL stands UC. JENNIE is by the desk. PAM DL, sitting, WENDY in the UL chair. HORACE behind large chair]

LADY CANTERVILLE. That's cold comfort, Cecil.

CECIL. *[Steps DS]* I checked with the station master. No one
   fitting Virginia's description or Sir Simon's was seen getting on
   a train.

HORACE. Don't expect a ghost to buy a ticket, do you?

LADY CANTERVILLE. What I can't understand is why Virginia
   would go.

MRS UMNEY. A spirit like Canterville Ghost can't make a person
   do anything against one's will.

VICAR. *[From off-left]* Mrs. Otis! Mrs. Otis!

WEEDS. That'll be the Vicar.

   [ALL look L, VICAR hurries in, out of breath.]

LADY CANTERVILLE. What is it, Vicar?

VICAR. She's back! She's coming this way.

LUCY. Thank heavens.

   [MRS DAMPIER follows the VICAR into the room]

MRS DAMPIER. Half the village is trailing behind her.

   *[MRS MUSGRAVE and MRS MIDWINTER enter from garden.
   MRS MUSGRAVE moves in front of table, L, MRS MIDWINTER
   stands beside WENDY. JENNIE moves R. VICAR stands by
   desk with MRS DAMPIER, leaving the French doors clear for
   Virginia's entrance. A pause for effect and then, VIRGINIA
   enters. She carries a small chest. CECIL crosses to her.]*

LUCY. Virginia, we've been worried to despair.

CECIL. You'd better come and rest.
   *[CECIL guides her to the sofa. LADY CANTERVILLE moves
   behind the sofa; LUCY steps DS]*

VIRGINIA. You shouldn't have worried. I was all right. I was with
   the ghost. *[She sits, CECIL beside her]*

WENDY. That's what we were worried about.

PAM. Where's Sir Simon?

VIRGINIA. *[Calmly]* Sir Simon is gone.

HORACE. Gone?

LUCY. Where?

VIRGINIA. To his sleep. He knows he was wicked, but he was really sorry.

HORACE. *[Points, sits in large chair]* What's that?

VIRGINIA. He gave me this chest of beautiful jewels before he went. *[She opens the lid. ALL strain to look, react as VIRGINIA holds up a fistful]*

MRS UMNEY. Beautiful.

LUCY. And so many.

MRS UMNEY. Rubies and pearls.

LADY CANTERVILLE. Diamonds. They're perfect.

VIRGINIA. I pleaded for him.

CECIL. With whom?

VIRGINIA. I promised Sir Simon I would keep it secret.

CECIL. You don't want to have any secrets from me?

VIRGINIA. I can tell you that thanks to Sir Simon I know what a precious thing life is.

PAM. Can I wear one of the bracelets?

WENDY. I want a ruby ring. That will make everyone at boarding school jealous.

HORACE. That's enough. Besides, the jewels belong to Lady Canterville.

LADY CANTERVILLE. No, Mr. Otis. The jewels are clearly Virginia's.

CECIL. I think if we took them from her, old Sir Simon would be out of his grave in a fortnight.

WEEDS. Raising the devil with all of us.

VIRGINIA. None of you understand.

JENNIE. What's to understand, Miss? He gave you a handsome present.

HORACE. Tidy fortune.

VIRGINIA. These jewels aren't for me. They're for all of us. For Canterville. Sir Simon sacked them from the village church, hundreds of years ago. He gave them to me so I could put them to use. *[She stands, holds out the chest.]* Here, Vicar. *[ALL react in surprise, look to VICAR who steps to VIRGINIA.]*

VICAR. *[Can't believe the good fortune]* You mean . . . you're giving them to me?

VIRGINIA. It was Sir Simon's wish.

VICAR. *[Takes the chest, still numb]* I've dreamed of something like this, but I never expected it to happen.

MRS DAMPIER. Children's Village can continue.

MRS MUSGRAVE. And Safe Harbor. Wait until they all hear the new

MRS UMNEY. A new roof for the church, too, Vicar.

VICAR. *[Overcome]* I know, I know. How can I ever thank you, Virginia?

VIRGINIA. It's the ghost you should thank.

MRS MIDWINTER. *[Looks into garden]* Look at that.

LUCY. What is it?

MRS DAMPIER. *[Amazed]* That withered old almond tree. It's in bloom.

JENNIE. Happened all of a sudden like, didn't it?

VIRGINIA. It means Heaven has forgiven Sir Simon.

CECIL. I guess we all owe him for something. If it weren't for the ghost, I wouldn't have met Virginia.

WEEDS. Let's hear it for Sir Simon.

[ALL cheer. During cheering, MADAM BALAKLAVA sweeps into the room from USC]

MADAM BALAKLAVA. Mr. Otis!

HORACE. *[Sighs]* Not again.

MADAM BALAKLAVA. I understand Sir Simon has vacated the premises.

LUCY. He has.

MADAM BALAKLAVA. In that case, you'll need another ghost.

HORACE. ANOTHER GHOST!

MADAM BALAKLAVA. So many of them are unemployed these days, and I'm partly to blame. I have several applicants for your consideration.

LUCY. We don't need another ghost.

LADY CANTERVILLE. I wonder what Sir Simon would think of this?

MADAM BALAKLAVA. Oh, but Lady Canterville. It was Sir Simon
   himself who made the suggestion before he 'crossed over.' He
   appeared to me in the costume of Robin Hood, which I thought
   was rather amusing and spirited of him. *[Calls USC]* Come in,
   please.

   *[Thunder. MARTIN THE MANIAC, LADY JOAN, HESTER
   and VAMPIRE DUCHESS enter fast and march down to MADAM
   BALAKLAVA]*

MRS MIDWINTER. Let's get out of here!

   *[MRS MIDWINTER, MRS MUSGRAVE, VICAR and MRS DAMPIER
   run out L. JENNIE and LADY CANTERVILLE exit USC. WEEDS
   and MRS UMNEY dash out DR. CECIL smiling happily, grabs
   VIRGINIA'S hand]*

CECIL. Come on, Virginia. You know too many ghosts as it is.

   *[He pulls her into the garden. HORACE, LUCY and PAM and
   WENDY look slightly stunned, but they carry on – they've
   learned to take English spectres more gracefully. MADAM
   BALAKLAVA, like a hostess at a tea party, makes introductions.
   HORACE stands.]*

MADAM BALAKLAVA. Martin the Maniac, may I present Mr.
   Horace Otis. From America.
HORACE. Delighted.
MARTIN. A pleasure sir. I've always wanted to visit the colonies.
   [They shake hands]
MADAM BALAKLAVA. Lady Joan the Graveless, may I present
   Mrs. Otis.
LUCY. Charmed.
LADY JOAN. I love your house.
MADAM BALAKLAVA. *[To LUCY and HORACE]* The Vampire
   Duchess.

HORACE. Delighted you could drop in.
DUCHESS. You're too kind.
HESTER. *[Crosses to the girls]* I'm Hester the Horrid.
   [PAM and WENDY stand]
PAM. Hi.
WENDY. Sir Simon may be gone, but his spirits linger . . . . !

   [Curtain]

THE END

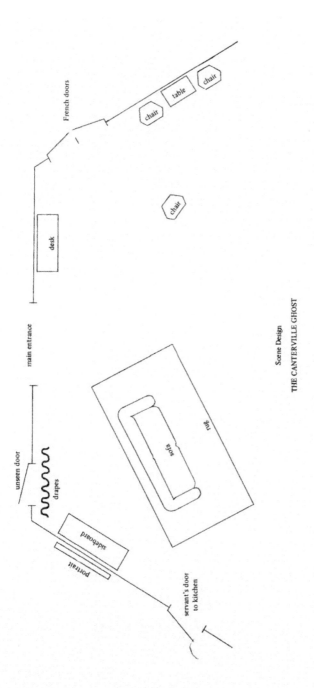

Scene Design

THE CANTERVILLE GHOST

MUSIC USE NOTE

Licensees are solely responsible for obtaining formal written permission from copyright owners to use copyrighted music in the performance of this play and are strongly cautioned to do so. If no such permission is obtained by the licensee, then the licensee must use only original music that the licensee owns and controls. Licensees are solely responsible and liable for all music clearances and shall indemnify the copyright owners of the play(s) and their licensing agent, Samuel French, against any costs, expenses, losses and liabilities arising from the use of music by licensees. Please contact the appropriate music licensing authority in your territory for the rights to any incidental music.

IMPORTANT BILLING AND CREDIT REQUIREMENTS

If you have obtained performance rights to this title, please refer to your licensing agreement for important billing and credit requirements.

Lightning Source UK Ltd.
Milton Keynes UK
UKHW021848120123
415233UK00015B/942